JOURNEY TO HAPPINESS

She looked at Hugh trying to tell him without words that she needed his kiss.

Instead he took her hand and held it between both his. After a moment, with her pulses racing as she wondered what he meant to do, he dropped his head and laid his lips against the back of her hand.

Then, without raising his head, he turned her hand over and kissed her palm with lips that seemed to scorch her. Pleasure travelled like wildfire up her arm and across her skin until she was trembling with delight.

Martina took deep breaths to steady herself against the power of such strong feelings. Surely now he would kiss her, as she yearned for him to do.

But he looked up at her. When he spoke it was in an unsteady voice.

"Forgive me," he said. "I gave you my word."

THE BARBARA CARTLAND PINK COLLECTION

Titles in this series

JOURNEY TO HAPPINESS

BARBARA CARTLAND

Barbaracartland.com Ltd

THE BARBARA CARTLAND PINK COLLECTION

Barbara Cartland was the most prolific bestselling author in the history of the world. She was frequently in the Guinness Book of Records for writing more books in a year than any other living author. In fact her most amazing literary feat was when her publishers asked for more Barbara Cartland romances, she doubled her output from 10 books a year to over 20 books a year, when she was 77.

She went on writing continuously at this rate for 20 years and wrote her last book at the age of 97, thus completing 400 books between the ages of 77 and 97.

Her publishers finally could not keep up with this phenomenal output, so at her death she left 160 unpublished manuscripts, something again that no other author has ever achieved.

Now the exciting news is that these 160 original unpublished Barbara Cartland books are ready for publication and they will be published by Barbaracartland.com exclusively on the internet, as the web is the best possible way to reach so many Barbara Cartland readers around the world.

The 160 books will be published monthly and will be numbered in sequence.

The series is called the Pink Collection as a tribute to Barbara Cartland whose favourite colour was pink and it became very much her trademark over the years.

The Barbara Cartland Pink Collection is published only on the internet. Log on to www.barbaracartland.com to find out how you can purchase the books monthly as they are published, and take out a subscription that will ensure that all subsequent editions are delivered to you by mail order to your home.

If you do not have access to a computer you can write for information about the Pink Collection to the following address :

Barbara Cartland.com Ltd.
Camfield Place,
Hatfield,
Hertfordshire AL9 6JE
United Kingdom.

Telephone : +44 (0)1707 642629
Fax :   +44 (0)1707 663041

THE LATE DAME BARBARA CARTLAND

Barbara Cartland who sadly died in May 2000 at the age of nearly 99 was the world's most famous romantic novelist who wrote 723 books in her lifetime with worldwide sales of over 1 billion copies and her books were translated into 36 different languages.

As well as romantic novels, she wrote historical biographies, 6 autobiographies, theatrical plays, books of advice on life, love, vitamins and cookery. She also found time to be a political speaker and television and radio personality.

She wrote her first book at the age of 21 and this was called *Jigsaw*. It became an immediate bestseller and sold 100,000 copies in hardback and was translated into 6 different languages. She wrote continuously throughout her life, writing bestsellers for an astonishing 76 years. Her books have always been immensely popular in the United States, where in 1976 her current books were at numbers 1 & 2 in the B. Dalton bestsellers list, a feat never achieved before or since by any author.

Barbara Cartland became a legend in her own lifetime and will be best remembered for her wonderful romantic novels, so loved by her millions of readers throughout the world.

Her books will always be treasured for their moral message, her pure and innocent heroines, her good looking and dashing heroes and above all her belief that the power of love is more important than anything else in everyone's life.

"What everyone needs and longs for is love, love, love – and not sex, sex, sex!"

Barbara Cartland

CHAPTER ONE
1883

A ball at Lady Bellingham's country house was always the height of elegance. Scented flowers adorned the ballroom and the orchestra was the best that money could buy.

The guests also were of the best in the land. The Bellinghams had many well connected neighbours and although the London Season was over, there were still aristocratic young ladies who hoped to find husbands as well-born as themselves. Or if not well-born, then rich.

Sir Hugh Faversham, whose own estate, Faversham Park, was about five miles away, was a mere Baronet, but his vast wealth made him acceptable to the very highest ranks.

It was now fifteen years since his first appearance in Society, but he was still single and still preferring bachelor pleasures to the joys of marriage.

Or so the world thought.

Only those who knew him best realised that he would have abandoned his self-indulgent life in a moment if only a certain lady would just smile on him.

But since the lady remained hard-hearted he had no choice but to fill his existence with idle pastimes for which he cared very little.

"I swear I have thrown every eligible *debutante* into his path," Lady Bellingham complained. "He flirts with them all, smiles at them all, dances with them all. And forgets them the next moment."

"You throw too many pretty girls into his path," her spouse advised her. "He has grown adept at side-stepping them."

"I told him once, frankly, it was time he thought of filling the Faversham nurseries. After all, he owes something to tradition."

"And what did he say to that idea?"

"He said 'what tradition?'" her Ladyship responded in accents of deep exasperation. "The title could die out for all he cares. I said, 'Really! After all the trouble his grandfather took securing it!' And he said that was *exactly* what he meant."

"Good for him! A man with his moneybags can say what he pleases."

"You are just impossible!"

"Anything you say, my dear."

Having completed his duty dances, Sir Hugh was walking around the ballroom, watching the whirling couples with an apparently careless eye.

In fact he was completely alert for any sign of his beloved entering the ballroom.

Several ladies tried to catch his attention, not only because he was wealthy, but because he was also a fine handsome gentleman in the prime of life.

His figure was tall and athletic and his face lean with regular features and a wide good-tempered mouth.

But Sir Hugh cared for only one lady and she was not present.

At last his patience was rewarded by the late arrival of

Lady Fayebourn, Miss Harriet Shepton and Miss Martina Lawson.

The two young ladies looked very much alike, both in their early twenties, tall and slender with glorious fair hair. They might have been sisters.

By far the prettier of the two was Miss Shepton. Her features were dainty, her eyes large and blue, her expression winning. Hers was a face to make men fall in love.

Miss Lawson was attractive, but the most notable characteristic in her face was her intelligence. Her eyes were keen, almost sharp, her chin resolute and there was nothing melting in her manner.

It was even rumoured that she was a blue-stocking. Horror of horrors! Here was a young woman who but for her comfortable dowry would have frightened the suitors away.

Yet it was Miss Lawson who made Sir Hugh's eyes soften as he looked at her. Miss Shepton was to him no more than a pretty doll.

He greeted all three ladies with great courtesy and attentiveness and procured ice creams for them. When he returned it was to find that Martina had vanished.

"Lord Perriwick asked her to dance," Harriet said.

"Ah, yes," muttered Sir Hugh displeased. "I know him and I believe he is greatly in debt."

"Fie, sir," Lady Fayebourn intervened archly. "You are always so hard on us poor ladies. Fancy saying that the only reason a man would want to dance with Martina was because he was after her money."

"I didn't precisely – "

"I own that she is no great beauty unlike dear Harriet here. But she is pleasant enough in her way, although I dislike a woman who displays her intelligence quite so blatantly, don't you, Sir Hugh?"

Sir Hugh thought that nobody could accuse Lady

Fayebourn of blatant intelligence, but he kept his opinions to himself.

As soon as possible he edged towards Martina, noticing how stunning she looked in an evening dress of pale rose tulle adorned with lattice panels of violet satin.

His intention was to ask her to dance, but he was foiled at the last moment by another partner, who whisked her away from under his nose.

For a while he had to content himself with watching her whirl about the room, thinking that no other lady looked so graceful and wishing her partner to perdition.

He consoled himself by dancing with Harriet. They knew each other slightly since Martina was staying at Harriet's nearby home, Shepton Grange, and he had danced with her before.

She was very pretty in pale yellow, although Sir Hugh's experienced eye was sure he had seen her in the same dress last season.

It was strongly rumoured that Harriet lived under the thumb of Rupert Ingleby, her stepfather. He had married Mrs. Shepton for her money and demanded every penny for himself, forcing his step-daughter to scrimp and save.

Martina lived with the family and had seen what was happening and had often told Sir Hugh that the rumours were true. On occasions like this he understood it for himself.

"I am delighted to see you here, Miss Shepton," he began as they danced. "I hope that your dear Mama is better these days?"

"I am afraid Mama is still an invalid," Harriet replied with a sigh, "and she always will be. My stepfather did not really wish me to come tonight. He said it was inappropriate but Mama said she liked to see me enjoying myself."

"She is right and I am very glad you allowed yourself

to be persuaded. How could Martina have come without you?"

"I couldn't let Martina down when she has been such a good friend to me," Harriet responded at once. "I don't know what I would do without her."

"I imagine that if your own social life is restricted, hers must be as well," he said, trying not to reveal just how interested he was in Martina's social life.

"Oh, yes, indeed," Harriet concurred. "But Martina is very fond of reading, you know. She says she would rather read a good book than talk nonsense to a gentleman any day!"

She made the remark quite unconsciously. It did not seem to have occurred to her that Sir Hugh might have a personal interest in her friend.

He wondered if Harriet thought that, at thirty-five, he was too old to aspire to Martina's hand. It was a demeaning thought.

"Does she consider that *all* gentlemen talk nonsense?" he asked mildly.

"She says most of them do and the great advantage of a book is that you can close it whenever you want, even in mid-sentence, without having to worry about hurting its feelings."

"That sounds so like Miss Lawson," he said appreciatively. "I can just hear her saying it."

The dance came to an end. Harriet's hand was immediately solicited by another partner, but Sir Hugh had to wait another half-an-hour before he could engage Martina's attention.

When he asked her to dance, she gave him a charming smile.

"Of course. How could any ball be complete if I didn't dance with my dearest friend?"

There was something depressing about the word 'friend' when he longed so much to be a closer relation. But it was better than nothing, he supposed.

As they danced Sir Hugh would have liked to give the conversation a sentimental turn, but Martina's mind was fixed on other subjects.

"I saw you dancing with Harriet," she said. "Did she seem to you in good spirits?"

"I am afraid not, but then I think she is never very lively. I understand that her home life is none too happy."

"You are so right, I fear. I have known it since the day I went to stay with her after her mother married that dreadful man."

Her face was grim as she continued,

"Mr. Ingleby, her stepfather, obviously disliked her from the first and is doing everything he can to keep her mother completely under his thumb. He would like to be rid of Harriet as soon as possible.

"He resents letting her have any money to spend, although it is really hers and her mother's.

"Poor Harriet has nobody to turn to except me. That is why I have stayed with her ever since to be what help to her I could. I would actually rather enjoy going back to live in my own little house in London, where there are so many memories of my dear parents. But Harriet was very good to me when I was unhappy and I must be there now when she really needs me."

Sir Hugh smiled.

"That sounds just like you, my dearest," he said. "You always try to help those who are in trouble and ignore your own problems."

"But I have no problems. I have enough money to live on and please myself, plus all the books I want to read. What more could I ask?"

"All the books you want?" he echoed, aghast.

"You have always known I was a blue-stocking!"

"But I don't think you should boast about it. Learning in a woman is all very well as long as she keeps it decently hidden, but actually to boast about it – my dear girl – really!"

She greeted this sally with a ripple of laughter.

"What a terrible man you are! Is that the correct way to speak to a lady?"

"It is the only way I can speak to you without sounding foolish. I have tried telling you that I am in love with you and want you to be my wife, but you were not impressed. In fact you have often forbidden me to mention the subject again."

"Yes, and you take no notice at all," she reproved him severely. "Despite my prohibition, you have just proposed to me yet again."

"Not really," he hedged. "I didn't exactly propose marriage. I merely reminded you that I had done so frequently over the past two years."

"Is that your way of telling me that you have now tired of me and will never propose to me again?"

"How I would love to be able to say yes," he sighed. "What pleasure it would give me to be free of your wiles!"

"But I exercise no wiles," she protested. "I wouldn't know a wile if it jumped out and said boo to me."

"I know and therein lies your attraction. You are undoubtedly the most totally honest and open person I know. You are completely without deviousness or tricks and it's those virtues which captivate me. And since a nature like yours will never change, I am condemned to remain ensnared for ever."

"You poor man! How I pity you."

"So you should, you heartless creature!"

They danced in silence for a while. Then he became aware that she was looking up at him through narrowed eyelids, behind which her eyes gleamed with fun.

"Do you really wish you were free of me?" she teased.

"You know quite well that I do not."

"Well I think you are very ill-advised to say as much, especially so often. My friend, you positively encourage me to ill-treat you. You should make me fear the loss of your love, give me some cause for jealousy, keep me guessing."

"Good advice, but too late for me," he sighed. "How can I keep you guessing about something you already know? And why should you fear the loss of my love when you don't want it?"

"But I might not want to let it go," she mused.

"My love is not a book to be put on the shelf until you are ready for it," he pointed out. "There is more to life than books, as one day you will find out."

"Do not belittle books – there is much to be said for them. They are so varied, so infinitely diverse. Unlike men, who are all exactly the same, bar a few unimportant details."

"It will come to this," he foretold gloomily. "You will end up marrying me because no other man will be able to endure you lecturing him."

"Well then, I shall end up by saying yes, which is what you keep saying you want?"

"But I had hoped you might marry me for love of myself alone, you see," he explained. "Or at least try to snare me for the sake of my money, like the others."

"That's how you approve of a woman behaving, is it?"

"No, but it's what they do whether I approve or not. I thought if you did it too, at least I would know that I had something you wanted."

"You don't fool me with this humble talk," she told

him severely. "You are far too used to females pursuing you. You take it all for granted and the minute one of us doesn't follow suit, you cannot cope."

"Not any one of them, just *you*."

"But you have always known that I will not marry you. How many times have I refused you?"

"I lost count when it got to five," he replied sadly.

"Then you should be well used to it by now."

"Too used to it. But I live in hope."

"Don't hope for me," she parried gaily. "I have decided never to marry. I am devoted to Reason."

"I know. You have told me so many times. But I want you to be devoted to me."

"I have made my decision in favour of Reason," she insisted with a decidedness that struck a chill into his heart.

"Could you not be devoted to us both?" he suggested.

She shook her head.

"Reason is a jealous lover. He leaves me no attention for anyone else."

"Then your life will be cold and lonely."

"But very interesting," she riposted.

Perceiving that she was in a mood where he could not reach her, he did not ask for another dance. Instead once they had parted, he sought congenial male company in the card room.

His attention was caught by a young man with a handsome face and dark brilliant eyes. He was sitting at the table concentrating on his cards in a fierce way that made Sir Hugh's heart sink.

As the game ended the young man threw his cards down in despair. But at once he began to prepare for another game.

"Robin, my dear fellow," Sir Hugh started, quickly claiming his attention. "Come and have a drink with me before you play any more."

Robin, Lord Brompton, looked up with his ready smile.

"Hugh, by all that's wonderful!"

He rose and strolled away with Sir Hugh. The two men took glasses from a tray proffered by a powdered footman and then walked out through the French windows into the night air.

"You talked about giving up gambling," Sir Hugh reproved him gently.

"I know but I thought my luck might have changed for just one last time."

"But it never does, you keep losing and your debts must be mounting up."

"You don't need to tell me," Lord Brompton sighed. "The plain fact is that I am so devilishly bored."

"But I heard you were about to become engaged."

"Hush!" Lord Brompton said hurriedly. "Don't go spreading that rumour. I am not engaged or even thinking about it, but the traps are closing in on me even as I speak."

Sir Hugh's dark eyes gleamed with amusement.

"I see. A bad case of a match-making Mama?"

"And a Papa, and all the aunts and an uncle! And it's not just a bad case, it could be terminal. Laura Vanwick is a decent girl in her own way, but I have no desire to marry her. If only I could persuade her family of that fact."

"Could you not flirt outrageously with another lady?"

"And then have another family trying to frogmarch me up the aisle," Lord Brompton replied, pale at the thought. "Thank you, *no*!"

"I only mentioned it because I have known you to have

enjoyed several light-hearted flirtations at one time – "

"Oh, flirtations!" Lord Brompton interrupted dismissively. "They come and they go and they mean nothing. What I would like is what you have, a woman who means so much that everything else pales into insignificance."

"The lady you refer to – whose name must not be mentioned – "

"Certainly not!" Lord Brompton was shocked. "I hope I know better than to bandy a lady's name around. And you should know better than to remind me."

"Your pardon, my dear fellow."

"It is just that you were once good enough to confide in me and nobody could miss the way you look at her."

"Unfortunately she does not return my feelings," Sir Hugh reminded him. "You need not envy me that much."

"But isn't it better to have loved and lost than never to have loved at all? Would you really choose not to have loved her, even if you never win her?"

Sir Hugh was silent for a moment.

"No," he said at last. "You are right. Even if I never win her, I have felt the joy of loving her and I certainly have not yet given up hope."

"And you will always harbour that hope until the day she marries another man."

"Do not say that," Sir Hugh said quickly.

"But it must be possible, unless you plan to carry her off by force."

"No, I am not planning anything excessive. I abhor a man who thinks he can win a woman by such methods. The lady I love must come to me gladly of her own free will and with a heart that is all mine. Anything less could only lead to misery for both of us."

To his great relief a noise from within the house enabled him to change the subject.

"Whatever is that commotion?" he demanded.

"It sounds like a man laughing," Lord Brompton observed.

"The creature making that row isn't a man, it's a hyena," Sir Hugh commented caustically.

Together they turned to return inside, just as Lady Bellingham came flying out.

"Do come and help me," she begged. "That dreadful creature, Rupert Ingleby, has arrived."

"My dear madam," Lord Brompton expostulated, "you should *not* have invited him."

"I couldn't help it. I wanted Miss Lawson and Miss Shepton, so I had to invite the whole family. Anything else would have been extremely rude. But I counted on him not coming, especially when the girls arrived with Lady Fayebourn."

"And he has suddenly turned up?" Sir Hugh asked.

"Yes, and even worse, he's brought an even more dreadful creature with him. His name is Brendan Muncaster and he is a factory owner!"

The loftily dismissive way she said 'factory owner' made Sir Hugh smile faintly. He knew, of course, that to a true aristocrat the scent of trade was anathema. But he had his own reasons for finding her remark amusing.

"May I remind you, madam, that my own grandfather made his fortune from factories," he said.

"That is quite different," Lady Bellingham brushed the objection aside. "You are clearly a gentleman – "

"Ever since my grandfather bought himself a title," Sir Hugh teased.

"I wish you wouldn't raise these irrelevant

objections," Lady Bellingham scolded him. "*You* do not have a red face, ginger whiskers and a voice like a banshee."

"My compliments, madam," Sir Hugh replied solemnly. "Most people wouldn't even know what a banshee sounds like."

From inside came a bellow of laughter that would have shattered glass.

"It sounds like *that,*" Lady Bellingham said acidly. "Now for pity's sake, the two of you, come inside and help me."

Inside they found Brendan Muncaster holding two glasses that he had seized from a footman. He quaffed one, next the other and then howled for more.

"A real drink this time! What was that stuff?"

"That stuff was the finest champagne," Lady Bellingham informed him, gimlet eyed.

Behind his hand Lord Brompton murmured,

"Not quite. The finest ran out an hour ago."

"Hush!" Sir Hugh muttered.

"Champagne is not a drink," Mr. Muncaster boomed. "Someone fetch me a proper drink. Brandy. Now there's something to seize a man's throat."

Lady Bellingham, who would have happily seized Mr. Muncaster by the throat, nodded to a footman, who disappeared.

"Not a bad little place you've got here?" Muncaster boomed. "I told my friend, Ingleby, I wanted to see the best place in London and he assured me that this is it."

If Lady Bellingham was flattered by this tribute she concealed it admirably.

"I'm building my own place, up North," Muncaster declared. "I'll make it like this, I think. Send me your architect. I'll pay him good money."

"Unfortunately the architect who created Bellingham House died three hundred years ago," his hostess informed him in a kind of suppressed shriek.

"That's a pity. He was a good man. On second thoughts I'd rather have something a bit more up to date. I've got the money to pay for it."

The footman had returned with a tray full of brandies. Muncaster seized two.

Seeing that Lady Bellingham was about to burst with rage and anguish, Sir Hugh took pity on her and moved forward. Rupert Ingleby, the man who had brought Brendan Muncaster to the ball, immediately pounced and introduced him as "my friend Sir Hugh".

Brendan Muncaster wrung him by the hand, breathed brandy in his face and shouted that any friend of Rupert Ingleby was a friend of his.

Whereupon Rupert Ingleby also wrung his hand and spoke of the entirely fictional good times they had apparently enjoyed together.

Ingleby was a burly man with mean little eyes that seemed to be sinking back into the flesh of his face. Like his friend his cheeks were ruddy with self-indulgence and he wore a corset in a vain attempt to disguise his paunch.

Sir Hugh had always thought of him as the most repellent specimen of humanity it had ever been his misfortune to meet. But that was before he met Brendan Muncaster.

He steeled himself to endure Ingleby's effusions, fortified by the sight, out of the corner of his eye, of Martina entering the room with Harriet just behind.

"And here is my daughter, Harriet," Ingleby broke off swiftly, turning to Harriet and drawing her forward so firmly that Martina was elbowed out of the way.

"*Stepdaughter*," Harriet murmured, regarding both

men with equal revulsion.

Sir Hugh edged his way around to Martina.

"That behaviour was the outside of enough," he fumed. "To shove you aside in such an ungentlemanly fashion."

"True, but it saved me from having to meet Mr. Muncaster and for that I would endure a great deal!"

"You are right," Sir Hugh agreed. "And if you dance with me, you will be further saved from meeting him."

She gladly swept into his arms and they joined in the waltz that was just beginning.

"Poor Harriet," Martina mourned. "Imagine how it must feel to have no escape from those two vulgarians. At the end of the evening she will be forced to go home with her stepfather. If it comes to that, so will I."

"Why was he so anxious to call her his daughter?" Sir Hugh wondered. "There's no love lost between them."

"Harriet is a lady and behaves like one," Martina answered wryly. "Maybe he is hoping some of her gentility will rub off on him if he claims kinship. Oh, look, there she is."

Glancing across the room Hugh saw Harriet dancing with Brendan Muncaster. On her face was a smile that seemed to be held on by force and her whole body displayed her reluctance.

'Poor girl,' he thought.

But then he banished her from his thoughts. He held his beloved in his arms and he was going to make the most of it.

So he smiled at her and rejoiced at the smile she returned as the music swelled and they whirled around the floor together.

CHAPTER TWO

Harriet awoke early next morning and rose to sit by her window watching dawn break over the grounds of Shepton Grange. The light touched the tops of the trees and then the stream in the distance, glittering in the early sun.

This had been her home for as long as she could remember. She had always loved it, but these days it no longer felt like her home.

Not since Rupert Ingleby had forced his way in and stayed.

Her heart was heavy when she remembered Lady Bellingham's ball the night before.

Her stepfather had shown himself in his least pleasant light. But there was no surprise in that, she thought. All his lights were unpleasant to a greater or lesser degree.

But last night he had produced a man shockingly like himself, a loud-mouthed vulgarian with mean eyes. The effect was doubly horrible.

She knew that Ingleby, who had run the house and the estate after he had married her mother, was well-known for being mean. He spent as little as possible on anyone but himself.

At one time he had been poor and now that he had succeeded in marrying money, he counted every penny, never giving away as much as a farthing if he could possibly help it.

Sadly, Harriet remembered her father, the Honourable Gavin Shepton and how generous he had always been, ever willing to share his wealth with others. He tipped generously, treated his servants well and lavished treats on his wife and child.

Harriet was sure that Ingleby had married her mother only because she was rich. Her mother always saw the best in him and insisted that he had married her for love.

But Harriet could never understand how Mama could possibly put another man in her father's place, especially when he had only been dead for little more than a year.

"I am lonely, darling," her mother had said. "I find it very difficult to go on living and running the estate without your father to guide me as he always did."

She was particularly at a loss when her daughter was at school.

"You must understand," she said, "that it's terrible for me to sit alone in that great house, which is so empty, except for the servants.

"When you are at school, how do you expect me to eat dinner alone and to sit until it is bedtime with no one to talk to and no one to discuss – as I always did with your father – what has happened today and what will happen tomorrow. Now I am completely and absolutely alone."

Then Rupert Ingleby appeared unexpectedly. He claimed to be an old friend of Gavin Shepton, but neither Harriet nor her mother had ever heard his name mentioned.

"If he ever knew him at all it was only as a brief acquaintance," Harriet had told her dear friend, Martina.

But in her loneliness Mrs. Shepton had invited him to the house several times and gradually Harriet realised that he was determined to stay for good.

Harriet's mother was not the kind of woman who

could live alone. Although she was forty, she was still exceedingly pretty and attractive to men. She wanted a man who loved her, who would protect her and relieve her from the responsibility of giving orders.

It became clear that Ingleby was all too ready to relieve her of that responsibility and to give her at least the illusion of being loved and protected.

Harriet loathed him and hated the marriage, but to begin with she had not realised that he was so dangerous.

Her home had changed completely from the place where she had lived and been so happy into what at times became nothing but a prison. Ingleby started to interfere almost at once.

"If you want to go to so-and-so," he would say, "I think it is a waste of time. We will stay here. I have no wish to be uncomfortable in a hotel when this house is so delightful and I sleep peacefully in my very large and comfortable four-poster bed."

It was the sort of remark which made Harriet wish to say that it was her father's house and as he was no longer here, it was her mother's and hers.

Perhaps because he knew that she could see through him, he disliked Harriet almost as much as she disliked him. He had moaned about the cost of keeping her at school.

"It is disgraceful that they should charge as much when they are only teaching girls and not boys," he had complained.

For almost the only time, her mother insisted on having her own way.

"The school has a very good reputation," she had told her husband. "I have always wanted Harriet to receive the best education possible and to meet girls of good family, who will be presented at Court and then be invited to all the best and most exciting parties in London."

He had yielded grudgingly and Harriet had gone to the best school. But he was forever grumbling about the bills.

It was only because Harriet had wept on her mother's shoulder, saying she needed a friend and someone to accompany her, that Martina had come into the household.

Harriet had first met Martina at school.

They had been great friends and just once in the holidays Harriet had stayed with her and her widowed mother in London.

It was at the end of that year that Martina's mother had died after a very cold winter which had sapped her health and strength.

It was then Harriet had said to her mother,

"Please allow me to ask Martina to come here and stay with us. She is so alone now that her parents are dead and she is not close to any of her relatives."

"Of course the poor girl must come to us," Mrs. Ingleby had agreed. "We must be very kind to her and help her forget her loss."

So Martina had arrived for a very long stay. At first she was desperately unhappy, weeping in Harriet's arms night after night. But eventually she recovered from her grief and expressed her passionate gratitude to Harriet, the dear friend who had taken her in.

"If ever there is anything I can do for you," she had said, "You have only to name it. Nothing will be too much trouble. Nothing in the world."

Rupert Ingleby was very displeased at the new addition to the household. He only accepted the arrangement when it became clear that Martina had inherited a comfortable sum of money and insisted on paying her own way.

Even then Harriet knew that he was always watching

the money her friend spent, as if it came from his pocket rather than hers.

When she was old enough to leave school to be a *debutante*, she recognised that he resented so much money being spent on the ball which her mother gave when she 'came out', even though Martina was sharing the expense, as it was her debut too.

"He puts up with it because he is hoping I will get married and be off his hands," she confided to Martina.

"And you probably will," Martina said warmly. "You are the prettiest of us all."

The coming out ball was a triumph for both the two young ladies. Gentlemen clamoured to dance with Harriet. Martina also had her success, quieter than Harriet's, but very real.

She was attractive but without Harriet's delicate prettiness. What drew men to her was not her looks but an indefinable 'something' in her nature and in the quality of her mind. She was not quite like other girls, although few people could have said why.

Sir Hugh Faversham had been at her feet almost from the first moment, but she did not boast about it, not wishing to make fun of a good man, as she was indeed very fond of him, even if she could not fall in love with him.

She pitied Harriet with all her heart and as she had told Sir Hugh, remained with her for her sake, although she could have returned home to her own little house. She would have enjoyed the independence but would not abandon her friend.

Three weeks after the ball Harriet received her first proposal of marriage. He was a boring man who had insisted on dancing with her on several occasions.

She had danced with him only because she was sorry for him. Although wealthy, he always seemed alone. At parties she had noticed that people fled from him because he was such a bore.

Amused, she told her mother about his proposal and her instant refusal.

Then to her surprise her stepfather intervened,

"Now you take my advice and get married as soon as you can. Men want their wives to be young and unspoilt. If you want to be happy the sooner you are walking up the aisle the better."

He had been furious when she had turned down this proposal and several others. Increasingly she was sure that he would seize any chance to be rid of her.

But she wanted to marry a man that she loved and who loved her. And so she found the courage to stand out against her stepfather, no matter how unpleasant he made himself.

But these struggles always upset her for Harriet's nature was gentle. Martina, who was far more combative, would have managed better.

Now as the sun rose and her maid arrived with hot water ready for her to start the day, Harriet thought again about the ball last night, and wondered wearily how long she would be condemned to share a house with this unpleasant man.

'If only my true love would appear,' she dreamt. 'Then I could marry him and escape. But until he does, I shall just have to put up with it.'

There was no sign of Martina in the breakfast room, but Harriet knew that she sometimes avoided eating with Ingleby.

He was there now, looking as though he was suffering from a hangover. He glanced up at she appeared.

"Your mother is feeling poorly," he told her.

"Then I will go to her at once."

Harriet sped upstairs and went quietly into her mother's room. Mrs. Ingleby was lying in bed, looking pale. Harriet, sitting down near the bed, took her hand.

"You must not be ill," she urged. "The house is empty and miserable when you are not downstairs. We miss you more than I can say."

"That is very kind, darling, but I mean to stay in bed for a while. Then your stepfather is going to take me to the sea. He wants us to go to Brighton where he says there is a very good hotel and the sea air will, I am sure, make me feel better than I feel at the moment."

"I cannot bear you to be ill, Mama."

Kissing her mother she left her to rest and returned to the breakfast room.

"I think Mama is feeling better," she announced. "But perhaps she ought to go to the sea as the doctor has suggested."

"It was I who suggested that idea," her stepfather remarked sharply, "and now I have something to say to you."

*

Martina had also spent the first part of the day musing over the events of the night before.

As she had predicted, they had been forced to accompany Rupert Ingleby home at the end of the evening.

Mr. Muncaster was also in the carriage, which led to them being very squashed, especially Harriet, who was so unfortunate as to have to sit beside him.

When they reached home Muncaster had come in, and Ingleby had pressed Harriet to stay downstairs and entertain him, but she had refused and fled upstairs.

It had taken Martina a long time to calm her down. She had not left Harriet's room until she was safely asleep.

She had slipped downstairs early that morning and

taken a cup of coffee in the breakfast room, making sure to leave quickly before her host arrived. It might not be a very polite action to take, but she could not help herself.

Rupert Ingleby drinking too much at the ball the night before was one thing. Rupert Ingleby suffering the ill effects the next morning was too much to be endured. He could suffer his hangover without her she decided.

Now Martina was sitting at an elegant little desk in her room, writing a letter. With her spectacles on her nose she looked very studious and severe. Just like a blue-stocking, in fact. Sir Hugh would not have approved!

Suddenly there was the sound of footsteps in the hall outside and the next moment Harriet burst into the room.

Martina looked up in alarm as her friend was clearly very upset. Harriet slammed the door and threw herself hysterically onto the sofa.

"You will hardly believe what has happened," she cried. "I can hardly believe it myself, yet it is true."

She spoke so violently that Martina removed her spectacles, rose from the writing-desk and sat down beside her on the sofa.

"Now what has upset you, darling?" she asked her friend. "You know we both agreed it was a mistake to pay too much attention to your stepfather. I think he only means half of the nasty things he says."

"I have every good reason to be upset," Harriet answered passionately. "In fact, I can hardly find the breath to tell you what he has now suggested. I think he must be mad. I hate him! *I hate him!*"

Moving even closer to Harriet, Martina said,

"Come along, darling, tell me all about it. I expect we can find an answer to anything he suggests. We have always prided ourselves that our two brains are considerably better than anyone else's, especially your stepfather's."

There was silence.

Then Harriet said in a voice which did not sound like her own,

"He has discovered a really clever way to be rid of me."

"To be – ?"

"The only thing I can do is to run away or kill myself!"

Martina stared at her. Then she said,

"Oh, come along, Harriet, you are exaggerating what your stepfather has said. Anyway as we have often agreed, his 'bark is worse than his bite'."

"If we thought that, we were wrong," Harriet replied. "He has found a way of ridding himself of me which is so terrifying I can hardly bear to tell you what it is."

Suddenly she burst out,

"Oh, Martina, you must help me. Save me I beg you."

"But save you from what?" Martina questioned.

"He has found a husband for me – a horrible, vile, repulsive creature. I would rather die than marry him."

"But who is this man?"

"You saw him last night. *Brendan Muncaster*!"

"That revolting – *him*?" Martina exclaimed in alarm. "Surely not?"

"He told my stepfather last night that he wanted to marry me."

"And even Mr. Ingleby would wish to be connected with such a man? Surely not."

"He wouldn't have to see him. Mr. Muncaster's factories are in the North. He would take me back there and I would have to live in the wilds of Yorkshire and never see London again."

"And he fell in love with you last night?"

"Love has nothing to do with it," Harriet responded bitterly. "He wants to marry a lady so that he can impress his friends. He knows he will never be accepted as a gentleman in London despite all his money.

"Mr. Ingleby claims that it's a good match because he is so rich, but I would be cut off from everything I have always known, married to a creature who disgusts me!"

"I cannot believe that your stepfather could be so cruel. I know he is an unpleasant man but – "

"He will do anything to be rid of me, so that I cost him no more money."

"Surely you only have to refuse?" Martina said. "No one can make you marry a man you have only met once, whom you obviously dislike."

"Of course I don't wish to marry him," Harriet replied. "I don't want him to touch me and certainly not to kiss me. And the idea of having his children makes me feel sick. Oh, Martina, what can I do?"

"You must refuse," Martina told her friend.

"But Step-Papa has already said yes," Harriet exclaimed. "Somehow he will force me, perhaps when I am unconscious, up the aisle and this man will take me away with him."

She was half out of her mind with despair.

Martina stretched out her hand.

"Now listen, my dear," she said. "We have to find a way of refusing this man. Your mother – "

"She cannot save me. She is too frail and ill. How can she contend with him?"

"Yes, of course, that could be disastrous when she is so weak," Martina agreed.

"It's no use," Harriet wept, "I have no hope."

"Now *that* I will not believe," Martina said robustly.

"There is always something that can be done if one is strong-minded."

"But I am not strong-minded," Harriet groaned in despair.

"However *I* am," Martina said firmly. "And I will *not* allow this marriage to happen."

"Oh, Martina, how strong and brave you sound! Do you really think you can do something?"

"I am quite certain of it. You can rely on me absolutely. You will not have to marry this man and together we will defeat your stepfather."

"How?" asked Harriet, awed by her friend's confidence.

"I am thinking of a great idea."

"Oh, yes. What great idea?"

"I don't know, I have not thought of it yet. But when I have, it will be the greatest idea to save you that anybody could possibly imagine."

"Will you please think of it soon?" Harriet urged anxiously.

"Not if you keep interrupting my thoughts."

"I am sorry."

There was a silence.

Then Martina said slowly,

"Yes, I *have* thought up an idea. I know exactly the way to deal with this problem. It may sound a rather strange notion to you, but it will succeed because it is so unexpected that nobody will believe it.

"What I have in mind is something that you may not like, but at least it is better than being forced into this terrible marriage."

Harriet drew in her breath,

"I will kill myself rather than let that happen."

"Then listen," Martina said. "This is what we have to do – "

*

Later that day Martina slipped out to the stables and ordered a pony harnessed to the dogcart so that she could drive herself cross country.

As she drove away she was aware of Ingleby watching her from behind the lace curtains.

Even without seeing his face she knew it would bear an expression of ill-will. There was no love lost between them. He knew she was Harriet's friend and would be campaigning against his plan.

'But you don't know exactly what I am going to do to thwart you,' she thought angrily.

In an hour she had crossed the countryside to Faversham Park and entered the great gate that led to an elegant avenue of poplars.

The beautiful mansion at the end of the drive looked like an ancient family seat, but Sir Hugh's grandfather had been the first of their family to own it. It was the fruits of trade, which Martina found as amusing as Sir Hugh.

As she drove up a groom came hurrying out to take the pony's head. Already the front door was being pulled open by an impressive-looking butler.

"Good morning, Miss Lawson," he greeted her. "Sir Hugh did not inform me that he was expecting you."

"Sir Hugh does not know I am coming to see him," Martina answered. "Is he in residence?"

"As it happens," the butler said, "he came in a quarter-of-an-hour ago. You will find him in the smoking room. Shall I announce you?"

"Thank you, but I will find my own way," she said,

hurrying down the passage, almost running, until she reached the smoking room.

She opened the door and stood for a moment looking at the figure seated at the desk, busy writing letters.

How good and kind he was, she thought. Such a safe, reliable friend. Who else could she have turned to in such an emergency?

Suddenly Sir Hugh looked up. Immediately he gave an exclamation of joy and jumped to his feet.

"Martina! How lovely to see you. I did not know that you were coming here today."

"I didn't know myself until an hour ago," Martina answered. "But I need help, my dear friend, and there is nobody I can trust as I trust you."

He took the hand which she held out to him and pressed his lips against it.

"You know that there is nothing I wouldn't do for you," he began. "You have only to command me, so do come and sit down on the sofa and tell me what is worrying you. But first, shall I send for some refreshments?"

"No, thank you. I have a great deal to tell you and I cannot think about anything else until I have done so. I need help desperately and you are the only one I could turn to."

She spoke so seriously that Sir Hugh looked at her in surprise.

Then he asked,

"What has happened? Tell me quickly. I hate you to be worried or upset."

"I am very frightened."

Sir Hugh looked at her in astonishment.

"What is frightening you?" he asked. "If it is a man I will knock his head off, if that is what you would want me to do."

"I want you to do much more than that."

Martina paused for a moment before she continued,

"Allow me to start at the beginning and then you will understand how difficult this situation has become."

She moved a little nearer to him as she spoke and slipped her hand into his.

His fingers tightened.

Slowly Martina started her story,

"Do you remember that appalling creature we met at the ball last night?"

"You mean the noisy character with the red whiskers and even redder face that Rupert Ingleby introduced?"

"Yes. None of us could imagine what he was thinking about to be trying to introduce such a monster into polite Society.

"But now everything is clear. The vulgarian is very rich and Mr. Ingleby is trying to force Harriet to marry him."

"Good grief! You cannot be serious!"

"I only wish I was not. But Harriet tells me everything and this morning she described Mr. Ingleby's disgraceful plans. Mr. Muncaster disgusts her, but all her stepfather can think about is being rid of her.

"I have promised to help her and I have come to you to beg you, if necessary on my knees," Martina cried, "to help her too."

Sir Hugh looked surprised but he did not interrupt as Martina resumed,

"She is already threatening to take her own life if I cannot save her."

"Are you really telling me the truth?" he asked. "Surely she has relatives and friends to prevent this happening."

"She has no one except me, as her mother is very ill. That is why I have come to you."

"But what can I do?" Sir Hugh wanted to know. "How can I prevent this marriage from taking place? I have no authority in the matter."

After an awkward moment Martina said,

"I have thought of an idea, but I am afraid to tell you what it is."

"Afraid?" Sir Hugh exclaimed. "That does not sound like you."

"Nevertheless it's true," Martina replied. "I cannot think of any other way that I can save Harriet from a fate worse than death."

"I understand that part," Sir Hugh said, "so tell me what it is."

Martina drew in her breath before saying,

"You may feel that I am asking too much."

"My dear girl, you are beginning to scare me. What can possibly be so terrible that you cannot tell me?"

"It is so difficult to suggest such an incredible idea – "

"Well, I am now expecting the worst and I can only hope it is not as bad as I fear."

"I think it may seem even worse," Martina admitted. "But it is the only way we can save Harriet."

"Very well. What is it?"

There was a moment's pause before Martina said in a low voice,

"*I want you to marry Harriet.*"

CHAPTER THREE

"What?" he screamed in thunderstruck accents. "Martina have you taken leave of your senses?"

"I warned you it was difficult – "

"Difficult! My dear girl, I think you must have gone completely mad."

"If you would only – "

"I know I said I would do anything for you, but that most emphatically does not include marrying another woman. What on earth would we say to each other? Or are you proposing to come and live with us as well? Shall the three of us enjoy a cosy little *ménage a trois* by the fireside in the evening?"

"I wish you would stop talking nonsense," Martina said crossly, forgetting for the moment that she was here as a supplicant.

"Nonsense? You come here with the most feather-brained scheme it has ever been my misfortune to hear, and you dare to accuse *me* of talking nonsense.

"Upon my soul, Martina, I used to think of you as a woman of intelligence. In fact, I once believed that you had more brains than were suitable in a young lady – "

"Oh, did you!" she retorted, incensed.

"Not any more, however."

"Of all the arrogant, thick-skulled, prejudiced men in the world, you are the worst. I just don't know why I ever bothered to come here."

"You came because you knew I was the one man in England who wouldn't have you put under restraint for such a lunatic idea."

"If you had listened to me," she seethed, "instead of shouting me down whenever I open my mouth, you would have known that all I was asking you to do was act a part, a part that only the most brilliant of men could act convincingly. I thought you *were* brilliant – "

"No, what you thought was that you had me so much under your thumb that I would fall in with any tomfool scheme," he riposted not mincing matters.

"I thought I could rely on you when you said that you loved me and would do anything for me," she said in tearful exasperation. "But I see now that I was mistaken. It was all meaningless talk. You are just like all other men."

"What do you mean, *all* other men?" he demanded. "How many other men have you known?"

"That need not concern you – "

"Well, it does concern me if I am to be asked to make a dashed fool of myself for your sake. I don't say I will not do it, but I would like a few explanations first."

"There is no need for explanations," Martina declared rising. "You have stated your position, sir, and I need not detain you further."

"Stop talking like an actress in a melodrama," he scolded. "And for pity's sake, turn off the waterworks. I know they are not for real. You are not a weepy sort of woman."

"You know nothing about me," she sobbed pathetically into her handkerchief.

"I said stop crying. It doesn't fool me for a second."

She stopped at once. He had been perfectly right.

"So now, tell me the worst," he said in a resigned voice.

"I want you to save Harriet by marrying her. But if we all play our cards cleverly, it will be a marriage which is not real."

"And if we *don't* play our cards cleverly?" he asked in an ominous voice.

"Never mind. We will."

"I do not understand," Sir Hugh pleaded.

"You have been kind enough," Martina asserted, "to ask me to be your wife on several occasions."

She smiled at him as she continued,

"What I am suggesting is that Harriet plays my part and you marry her with everyone, including the priest, believing that she is me."

She saw him looking at her with an appalled expression and added quickly,

"It is really very simple."

"I am glad you think so."

"You marry Harriet. She will be dressed in my clothes, wearing rather a heavy wedding veil, so that even her best friend would not realise it was her and not me. It is the perfect way for Harriet to get away from her stepfather.

"It will be a very hasty wedding because we don't want anyone to realise anything unusual has taken place."

"Not – realise that anything – unusual – " Sir Hugh echoed in a slow, stunned voice.

"We will announce that, as you are so anxious to travel abroad on a special mission, the wedding has to take place quietly in your private Chapel."

"I think I *will* have you placed under restraint," he growled in a hollow voice.

"Do please be serious. It is really all very simple."

"Why do I become more worried every time you say that?"

"I cannot think. You have absolutely no cause. You will be marrying my friend, but with my name. Then everyone will think I am the bride, but actually Harriet will be. When this is later discovered or we announce it to those who are interested, you will find that your marriage is completely illegal."

She smiled as she added,

"Since you will have married a woman with a false name, you will not be married to her in any sense. In fact, the whole marriage will be null and void."

"And in the meantime I will have told a lot of lies that will ruin me."

"No one need know that this has happened except the close family," Martina asserted. "And if you introduce Harriet to some charming man when you are away on your honeymoon, she will eventually be happily married to someone she really loves."

"We are going to have a honeymoon?" he asked wildly.

"Of course. That is how you take her away. Naturally I will come with you. It's quite the custom for a bride to take a friend on her wedding trip, so the three of us will travel together on your yacht."

"Oh, we go abroad, do we? Do the two of you have passports?"

"We do. Harriet travelled abroad with her parents the year before her father died. And Mama and I planned to take a trip and prepared everything, including obtaining passports, but then she died before we could leave.

"So you see," she concluded with an extravagant gesture, "I have thought of *everything*."

"You have thought of nothing that matters," he informed her gloomily, "including the scandal that you are preparing for us all."

"There will be no scandal. We will just enjoy a nice little trip together. If we two girls find it impossible to amuse you, you may throw us off at the first stop your yacht makes and we will be obliged to find our own way home."

There was silence.

Then quite unexpectedly Sir Hugh laughed.

"I have had many extraordinary ideas suggested to me in my life, but this is the best. I have never heard of anything more ridiculous than that I should pretend to marry you, marry Harriet instead and then take the pair of you on honeymoon!"

"I will stay at home, if that is what you wish," Martina replied. "But I do think it will do us all good to leave England behind."

"Do you really think we can get away with such an outlandish scheme?"

"Of course we can, as long as we tell as few people as possible what we are doing. The one person who would really be interested is, of course, the villain of the peace. He will be trying to procure Harriet's money entirely for himself."

Martina smiled as she continued,

"But you must be very discreet. It is too good a story and some people would tell their best friends, who would tell the world.

"In fact, the whole County would soon be saying you had done Harriet's stepfather down and he jolly well deserved it."

"And there aren't any unforeseen complications?" he demanded suspiciously.

"How could there be?" she responded airily. "If you are married to someone who gives a false name, the marriage is annulled and you will again be as free as you are now."

Sir Hugh thought for a moment before suggesting,

"It would be much easier if I could marry you as I have always wanted to do."

"I know," Martina answered. "But I could never be happy if I thought that Harriet, who has never done anyone any harm, is being made so wretched."

"You are right," Sir Hugh agreed quietly, "of course you have to save the poor girl."

"You do understand," Martina said. "I knew you would. Please say you will do it. If Harriet is free from the terrible threat hanging over her, then perhaps we can all be happy."

"Does that include me?" Sir Hugh enquired.

Martina nodded.

"Of course it does. You will have not only saved Harriet from killing herself, but me from feeling that if she does, I could somehow have prevented her. Then we will all be very happy in the future."

"How does that include *me*?" Sir Hugh quizzed her again.

Martina knew what he was asking. There was a moment's pause before she said,

"First things first! We have to save Harriet and I cannot think who else I could go to for help."

"Naturally I want you to come to me rather than anyone else," Sir Hugh told her. "I look forward to our trip on my honeymoon if you are taking part in it – even if it isn't the way I pictured us honeymooning together."

Martina's eyes twinkled.

"You always get your own way. You were determined, when you acquired that yacht, to take me away on it and now it's going to happen."

"But I didn't mean it to be like this, I thought that you and I would be alone on the yacht and I would tell you a thousand times a day how much I love you.

"Now we will have with us my pretend bride – or are you my pretend bride? Already I've lost track – anyway, there will be three of us and that is going to make it very difficult and not as wonderful for me as I had hoped."

"Please don't say any more," Martina begged him. "Just now I cannot think of anything but saving Harriet."

"I understand, my dear, and I think you are very clever to have thought of this mad scheme. But don't forget that I am not doing this for Harriet. I am agreeing to it because I love you and want you."

He spoke very positively and his eyes held hers until she looked away.

Suddenly Martina was blushing which surprised her. Sir Hugh had never made her blush before.

Martina rose hastily to her feet.

"I must return," she said. "But before I go, promise you will do as I ask. Let me go with an easy mind, I implore you."

Sir Hugh did not speak, but stood looking at her with his heart in his eyes.

"Please," she begged. "I have nowhere else to turn."

"If I do this mad thing, will you definitely promise to come on this 'honeymoon' too?"

"Of course I will. Since you and Harriet hardly know each other, it will be very difficult for you to pretend to be happily married unless I am there to put you at ease with each other."

"Will the pretence have to be kept up for long?" Sir Hugh asked.

"That is up to you – we have to be sure that Harriet is safe before we can tell anyone the truth."

"But how will we know when she is safe?"

"When the dreaded Muncaster has gone back North or married someone else."

"At which point Rupert Ingleby will produce another suitor," Sir Hugh pointed out. "Are we all to live in hiding forever?"

"Of course not. I will set up my own establishment and she can hide with me. I will think of something."

"You have not thought this out properly," he retorted with an attempt at sternness.

"Well, I haven't had very much time," Martina defended herself. "Besides, the greatest Generals go into battle prepared to improvise. Think of Napoleon. Think of Wellington."

"What about them?"

"Well – think of them."

"I am thinking of them and I know that they would both have had too much sense to become involved in an escapade like this. I also know that neither of them ever approached a battle in a spirit of '*I'll think of something.*'"

"But we cannot see that far ahead."

"I can," he said gloomily. "I can see myself ending up married to both of you at once. I see bigamy charges and a prison sentence. Why did I ever allow myself to listen to you?"

"Because you are a good and kind man."

"Do not start that," he begged. "I warn you, don't talk to me like that. It's not playing fair."

"I promise you that as soon as possible we will bring

it all to an end," Martina soothed him. "And then we can tell everyone who is interested the truth that you are not married and I remain what I am now, your admirer and your friend."

"You know as well as I do what I want you to be."

"We will talk about it later. For the moment you have to act the part of the blissful bridegroom and earn my eternal gratitude."

"If you ask me, I think you are making me a complete and utter fool. How can you really expect me to act the part of a bridegroom to a woman I barely know, and to use your name for the marriage, when I actually want *you* to be my wife."

"It is only acting," Martina asserted. "I could not marry you or anyone else if I thought Harriet would kill herself in preference to marrying a man she dislikes. She would rather die than let him touch her."

Martina spoke so violently that for a moment Sir Hugh stared at her.

"If I had any sense I would make you promise to marry me in return for helping you."

Martina looked at him strangely.

"No," she said. "You would never do that. You are too honourable to blackmail me in such an underhand way."

Sir Hugh turned away, cursing under his breath.

"You are right," he grumbled at last. "Not about me being honourable because I am not. But I would never try to make you marry me by such methods. I want you to marry me because you really want to."

"Oh, my dear," she sighed, "I can only give you the same answer I have given you before. I have no wish to marry anyone at the moment. But if you help me, I will be ready to show my gratitude one way or another."

"I need more than that," Sir Hugh stressed.

"Dear Hugh, I can make no promises. But once Harriet's problems have been solved, I can begin to think about myself."

There was silence and then Sir Hugh remarked,

"I suppose I shall have to be content with that."

"But I do thank you from the bottom of my heart."

"That is indeed what I want," Sir Hugh enthused, "your heart. Once you have saved Harriet then perhaps you can think of saving me from being so unhappy without you."

Martina looked at him and her eyes softened.

"You are being exactly as I thought you would be," she told him. "Kindly and understanding."

Then Sir Hugh did something she had never known him to do.

He lost his temper.

"Dammit, Martina! I am not kindly and understanding. I am a man deeply in love. I don't want to be kind to you, I want to kiss you. I want to marry you and make love to you and have children with you.

"Like a fool I will do whatever you ask of me, because it gives me the prospect of your company and I am desperate enough to pick up the crumbs from your table. *But I am not being kind.*"

Martina stared at him, astounded by the fierce light burning in his eyes. This was Hugh as she had never seen him, wrought to the point of madness by his love for her.

"Hugh, please – I didn't mean – "

But she got no further. With a growl of, "oh, the devil!" he reached out and pulled her into his arms. The next moment Martina found herself being fiercely and thoroughly kissed.

He had never treated her any way but gently before this moment, but there was nothing gentle about the ruthless embrace to which he was subjecting her now.

Martina made a feeble effort to struggle, but the arms holding her were like steel. Hugh was determined to kiss her and he was ignoring her objections in the most impolite way.

What dismayed Martina most was the feeling that her pulses had begun to race. Instead of being properly outraged she found herself growing warm and being forced to fight off her desire to press closely against him.

It was shocking. She must freeze him off at once, dismissing him from her presence with a well-chosen snub.

But that could be awkward when she had come to seek his help.

Put like that it became a positive duty to allow him a little freedom. So she permitted him to kiss her for a few moments longer, trying to ignore the fact that her heart was thumping in a strange way that had never happened to her.

When at last he lifted his head there was a new light in his eyes. It might almost have been one of triumph she thought. He was breathing hard and raggedly.

"Do you not want to slap my face?" he asked in a voice that shook.

"That would be very foolish of me when I need your help," she replied in a voice that also shook – to her great dismay.

"Is that the *only* reason, Martina?"

She flung him a look of reproach and he immediately backed off.

"Forget I said it. It was boorish and ungentlemanly. In fact, forget the whole thing ever happened."

Now he was being unreasonable she thought crossly. How could she forget such an event when her heart was still pounding?

"You need have no fear," he said heavily. "It will not happen again."

"Hugh – "

"I give you my word, on my honour as a gentleman, not to use your troubles as an excuse to force unwanted attentions on you. You may rely on me."

"Thank you," she replied in a small voice.

With her nerves still quivering with a perplexing new excitement, she was not quite certain that she wanted to rely on his word, but this was hardly the moment to say so.

"I shall – leave and start – the preparations," she stammered.

"And I shall do whatever is necessary here."

He showed her to the waiting dog cart. At the last minute she thought he would raise her hand to his lips, but he only closed the door and walked into the house without a backward look.

*

On the way back to Harriet's home Martina reflected that as it was midday, Rupert Ingleby would very likely be either riding or enjoying himself with some of his friends. So she would have Harriet to herself.

She hurried straight upstairs to Harriet's room and closed the door before saying urgently,

"I bring news that will make you happy!"

"Nothing could make me happy now," Harriet responded. "My stepfather came in just now and told me that Mr. Muncaster is coming here this evening. He wants to arrange for the wedding to take place this week."

"You are not to worry," Martina urged firmly. "I have a plan that will save you."

"Nothing can save me. I shall kill myself! When they

come to take me to the Church, they will find me dead in my bed!"

"You are not to talk like that," Martina scolded her. "You know that it is wicked and wrong to kill yourself.

"Now listen to me. You must allow your stepfather to believe that you have accepted the inevitable."

"But how can I? Even to think of that terrible man touching me makes me want to scream."

She reached out her hand and touched Harriet's lips.

"Be quiet," she said and listen to me. "Do you remember me telling you secretly that Sir Hugh Faversham wants to marry me? I have been to see him and he has agreed to help us."

"But how?"

"Tomorrow morning I will take you very early to Sir Hugh's house. There in his private Chapel you will go through a marriage ceremony.

"It will not be a real marriage. You will be heavily veiled and nobody will know it is you. When you begin your vows you will give your name as mine.

"There will be no reception. You will leave his house at once and travel to his yacht and the three of us will sail away together.

"Eventually we will reveal our little deception. The marriage will be declared null and void and you will be free. Best of all we will be well away from England when the bomb goes off and your stepfather realises that he has been thwarted."

"Oh, darling Martina, how kind you are to take so much trouble for me."

"What I think you should do and do it quickly is to draw as much money from your bank as you can. Then you must collect what clothes you think you will need on the yacht and be ready to bring them with you when we set out tomorrow morning."

"How can Sir Hugh be so kind? Of course he is doing it for you, but how deeply he must love you even to think of doing it. He sounds a wonderful man."

Martina laughed and to her own ears her voice sounded a little shaky.

"Perhaps *you* will fall in love with him," she said lightly, "or he with you and that will serve me right for keeping him waiting so long."

As she said these words she was assailed by the memory of Sir Hugh's lips on hers, with a hint of danger that had been so mysteriously exciting.

"Perhaps you'll become jealous," Harriet teased, "and when he next asks you will hurry to accept."

"Never," Martina declared decisively. "You should never allow a man to claim the upper hand – or, at least, you should never let him know that he has it.

"It is far more likely that he will find you so attractive that he'll beg you, on his knees of course, to make your marriage legal."

"And you would not object?" Harriet asked.

"Certainly not," Martina said decisively.

"Oh, Martina, I am so very grateful to you and Sir Hugh for saving me from that horrible man."

"Forget him. We are going to have an exciting time on your pretend honeymoon. You never know what might happen unexpectedly to you and of course to me."

Harriet laughed.

"Well, one thing makes me very happy," she said, "and that is that if I have to go on a honeymoon I want you to be with me."

Martina smiled at Harriet.

"Think how angry any real husband would be if when he wanted to be alone with his wife, there was another woman chatting away all the time. And because she is a woman she would be trying to attract his attention."

"That is very true, I had not thought of that," Harriet replied. "A honeymoon should be for only two people, a man and a woman."

"Your honeymoon will start off with two women and one man. "I am only praying that a handsome man will arrive and the pretend honeymoon will become a real one."

"You are asking for far too much. I have come to the conclusion that I am very unlucky and nothing I touch will ever come right."

"Nonsense," Martina rebuked her. "You must not fall into such a gloomy way of thinking just because you have encountered a few problems.

"You are now twenty and I am twenty-one. I think we can both sit looking up at the stars and hoping that one of them will fall into our laps and we will live happily ever afterwards."

Harriet drew in her breath.

"Do you really think that will come true?" she asked.

"Of course it will," Martina replied. "We will be so happy because we have been forced to struggle to find what everyone wants."

"What is that?"

"Love," Martina answered. "Love that comes from the heart and the soul. That is the love which sooner or later you and I are going to find."

As she spoke she bent forward and kissed Harriet on her cheek.

"Now hurry up, darling," she said, "and pack all the things you will want. Your clothes will need to be very carefully arranged so that your veil hides your face, and the priest can say afterwards he had no idea that the bride had disguised herself.

"It was only when you drove away on your honeymoon that the bridegroom found, to his surprise, and you might add, to his horror, that he had been married to the wrong woman!"

"It is so very, very kind of him to do this. What can I say to you, Martina, except that you are the most wonderful friend anyone could ever have?"

"You must keep your thanks until we are safely away from England on Sir Hugh's yacht. Now, instead of wasting time talking, you must start packing. Take your best clothes, the ones which make you look attractive and I will do the same. After all, we do not get married every day and when we do, we want to look exactly as a bride should look – beautiful, desirable and very, very lovable."

"You sound so confident," Harriet sighed wistfully. "I could never dare attempt such an adventure without you."

"We must make the most of it," Martina said, "and however long we live, we will make quite certain that everyone who is told our tale is astonished that we dreamed up anything so exciting."

Harriet laughed again.

But Martina knew that her eyes were shining and she looked very different in every way from when she had arrived.

'I have won! I have won!' she thought to herself.

But then she checked herself.

'No, I must be sensible. I have won only the first skirmish. The real battle to save my poor dear friend is only just beginning. But I will not be defeated. With Hugh's help we are going to be successful.'

CHAPTER FOUR

They spent the next few hours in Harriet's bedroom packing up her best clothes. Martina concentrated on finding material for two wedding veils which when she and Harriet wore them would make them look like each other.

"One of us is the bride and the other is the bridesmaid," Martina explained. "It is quite common for them to dress in a similar style, so that they harmonise."

"Even to the bridesmaid wearing a veil?" Harriet wanted to know.

"No, not exactly, but we will just look a little eccentric, nothing more."

"But suppose the priest is suddenly suspicious and makes us take off our veils?"

"We will just have to throw a fit of modesty and collapse in giggles," Martina improvised hastily, "but I hardly think that will happen. It simply is not done to treat a bride with suspicion. And the priest will find it difficult to see much in Sir Hugh's gloomy Chapel."

"I didn't realise he had one."

"It's very nice," Martina told her, "except for being rather dark. But that will be useful for our purpose."

When they had finished packing, they pushed the boxes against the window so that the thick silk curtain hid them.

"Now," Martina said, "it is most useful that I have always paid my own way, because I have my own horses and my own servants, who are loyal to me and not to Mr. Ingleby. I am going to send Thomas, my coachman, to the bank to draw out a large sum of money for me. Since your account is held in the same branch, he might fetch some for you too."

"Yes, indeed. I will write the letter now. You think of everything, Martina. I cannot tell you how grateful I am."

"Keep your thanks until we are safely at sea," Martina answered. "Just keep praying that nobody guesses what we are up to and then we can begin to dance and sing."

"Are you certain we'll get away?" Harriet asked nervously.

"Thomas will carry our luggage downstairs as soon as he can. Tomorrow morning at five o'clock we will drive away before anyone has the slightest idea we are even awake."

She was as good as her word, slipping down to the stables, drawing Thomas aside and giving him the letters to the bank.

He was gone for two hours returning with enough money for them both to be able to pay their own expenses while they were abroad.

To Martina this was most important. She recognised how much she was imposing on Hugh already. She did not wish either herself or Harriet to be a charge on him as well.

Then she explained to Thomas what she required on the following day.

"We want to drive straight to Sir Hugh's house with all the luggage," she said. "As you realise, Thomas, I am putting all my trust in you."

"You can rely on me, miss," he replied. "I've known you ever since you were born and I feels as if I belongs to your family and they belongs to me."

"Thank you very much, Thomas."

She slipped away from the stables and up the back stairs to Harriet's bedroom. They were both dreading the evening ahead when Mr. Ingleby might bring Mr. Muncaster to dinner, but instead he took him to dine with some friends nearby.

He gave as his reason the fact that his wife was ill, but Martina suspected that he was afraid that Harriet would throw his plans into disarray by being hostile to her unwanted suitor. As, indeed, she would.

While they were having dinner they knew that their luggage was being moved, but they did not speak about it in front of the servants. They could only hope silently that all was going well.

"I do not think," Martina said, "that Mr. Ingleby will be very late coming home. When his friends have 'enjoyed' Mr. Muncaster's company for a while they will be anxious to be rid of him. So let us retire early so as to avoid him. Also, we still have to finalise our wedding veils. I am sure your mother wore one when she married your Papa."

"Yes, of course she did," Harriet agreed. "I believe it was very fashionable at one time to wear long wedding veils of white lace with a headdress of flowers. Mama's is in her bedroom."

"Can you find it?" Martina asked.

"I'll try," Harriet promised. "She should be asleep by now."

They walked to Mrs. Ingleby's bedroom and Martina stood outside while Harriet tip-toed in. She found as she had expected that her mother was fast asleep.

Her tiaras, her wedding veil and several ornaments she had worn at the County balls were kept in a separate compartment of her wardrobe.

Harriet took everything on the shelf, even though it

meant going back twice. Then they carried it all up to Martina's bedroom.

To their delight there was enough heavy white lace for two veils.

What Harriet's mother had worn at her first wedding was a crown of flowers of different colours sprinkled with diamante so that they shone in the light.

"It's very pretty," Martina commented, "but why did she need two?"

"It was so like Mama," Harriet replied. "She thought one might get damaged or not be as becoming at the last moment as she wanted. So she insisted, so she told me, on buying two headdresses."

She sighed.

"I don't like taking them like this, but I know that if I could explain to Mama she would understand. She would do anything she could to help me escape this terrible marriage."

Swiftly Martina altered the two headdresses to look almost exactly the same. The veil which was intended to cover the bride's face until she was actually married was so large that she was able to cut it into two pieces.

One for herself and one for Harriet.

"So you are going to be a bride as well as me?" Harriet asked.

"We have to make it difficult for the priest to realise what is happening," Martina answered. "It will be dark first thing in the morning with only a faint light coming from the candles on the altar.

"The Bishop, when he finally comes to hear about the wedding, will discover that the marriage service was so muddled that therefore neither you nor I are actually married to Sir Hugh."

Harriet stared at her. Then she gave a cry.

"Oh, darling!" she exclaimed. "How did you think of anything so clever? Then of course we will both be free."

"We have to be very careful however not to let the priest suspect the muddle that is going on," Martina suggested. "Otherwise he will insist that the ceremony takes place again. Luckily, I think he is a very old man, who probably has poor eyesight."

"But surely we require my stepfather to believe in the marriage?"

"Of course – for a while. Just long enough to be rid of Muncaster. The Bishop can declare it annulled later."

"But will either of us actually be married to Sir Hugh?"

Martina considered this possibility.

"I suppose we will both be half married to him," she mused, "but as the law says that is impossible, both marriages will be invalid."

"Oh, Martina, you're so brilliant. Can we really carry it off?"

"We can if we get a good night's sleep," Martina replied firmly.

They were tucked up in bed nearly two hours before Mr. Ingleby returned. Harriet heard him talking to one of the servants waiting for him.

She fell asleep with her fingers crossed.

*

It was Harriet who woke first in the early dawn.

She awakened Martina and they talked to each other in whispers while they dressed in the pretty gowns they had chosen to wear for the wedding.

They carried in their hands the veils and headdresses they had arranged so skilfully the previous night.

51

When finally they crept silently downstairs and out through the back door, they found the carriage waiting for them with their luggage piled on the back.

They climbed in quietly, whispered to the coachman and he set off. It was a very bright morning and the sun was rising in the sky.

Martina knew that as Harriet looked back at the house which had been her home ever since she was born, she was saying goodbye to her mother whom she had always loved.

She had left a letter to say she was going away but would send her news when she could.

Then as they crossed the boundary of the estate, Harriet gave a cry of happiness.

"We've got away," she said excitedly.

"There is still a lot to do before you are really free," Martina told her. "You must not count your chickens before they are hatched!"

"I will do anything you want me to do."

"Just remember to keep the veil over your face and if you have to speak you must try to answer in a voice unlike yours."

After a moment Martina added reflectively,

"After all, Hugh is being very kind in helping us, but he does not want to find himself *married* at the end of this strange ceremony."

"I think he wouldn't mind if he found himself married to *you*," Harriet remarked slyly.

"But that would leave you free to marry Brendan Muncaster," Martina pointed out.

Harriet gave a cry of horror.

"Anything but that. I only mean that for you and him it might be the perfect match."

"Hmm!"

"I beg your pardon?"

"I said *Hmm!*"

"What does that mean?"

Martina sighed.

"It means I may have started something I do not know how to finish."

They drove on in silence.

As they reached the large and impressive house which belonged to Sir Hugh, Harriet slipped her hand into Martina's saying,

"It is all so frightening, please help me not to make any fatal mistakes."

"Just follow me," Martina encouraged her. "Remember everything depends on confusing the priest."

A servant was waiting just inside Sir Hugh's front door, ready to guide them to a small ante-room next to the Chapel.

There Martina and Harriet quickly changed into the wedding gowns they had brought with them.

Martina arranged one of the veils on Harriet's head and Harriet arranged the other one on hers.

There were flowers and diamante decorating the top of their heads, while it was difficult through their veils to see their faces.

Sir Hugh met them at the door of the Chapel.

"Are you still set on going through with this, Martina?" he addressed one of the veils.

"I am Martina," said the other veil. "That's Harriet.

"I beg your pardon. Are you really sure you want to go through with this wedding?"

"Of course," Martina replied indignantly. "Oh, please don't tell me you've changed your mind."

"I think this is a mad, ill-judged affair that is headed for disaster," he retorted bluntly. "But no, I have not changed my mind. I am going ahead only because, if I didn't, you would think up something even more outrageous and I might not be around to save you from disaster. Now, Miss Shepton, let us proceed."

He drew Harriet's arm through his and opened the door leading into the Chapel.

Inside there were bouquets of spring flowers with candles on the altar. The whole Chapel looked very attractive, but as there was no light except from the candles, it was difficult to see anything very clearly.

Both clad in white, both glittering with diamante, the two girls entered the Chapel itself to find the priest waiting at the altar.

Hugh led Harriet up to him with Martina following behind.

It was as the service began that Martina became aware of how Hugh had been very astute in his choice of priest. The man was at least eighty years old and although he wore glasses he still seemed very myopic.

As the two girls moved side by side, it was obvious that he was not certain, as they both looked exactly the same, who was the bride.

He cleared his throat and began the service,

"Dearly beloved, we are gathered together – "

It seemed to take him forever to come to the point, but at last he intoned,

"Hugh, wilt thou take this woman to thy wedded wife, to live together?"

And Hugh solemnly replied, "I will."

Martina held her breath as the priest continued,

"*Martina, wilt thou take this man to thy wedded husband?*"

And Harriet duly replied, "I will."

"*Who giveth this woman to be married to this man?*"

Hugh's secretary, who had been standing behind making notes, stepped forward to perform the duty.

Next Hugh took Harriet's hand and declared,

"*I, Hugh, take thee, Martina to my wedded wife, to have and to hold.*"

As she listened Martina did spare a thought for what this performance must mean to poor Hugh. He had dreamed of standing before this very altar with herself, saying these very same words. And now he was doing so, but with another woman.

She listened to see if she could detect any trace of a tremor in his voice, but he sounded solid and confident.

It occurred to her that perhaps he did not mind very much after all.

Then it was Harriet's turn to speak, murmuring softly to hide the fact that she had substituted her own name for Martina's.

"*I, Har-riet, take thee, Hugh to my wedded husband, to have and to hold –* "

When the speech had finished the priest looked down at his book and seemed to lose his place.

While his attention was thus occupied, Harriet stepped quickly back and Martina moved forward to stand at Hugh's side.

The priest was now ready to proceed. With his second bride beside him, Hugh took her hand in his and said,

"*With this ring I thee wed, with my body I thee worship and with all my worldly goods I thee endow.*"

His voice was low and deeply moving and a strange

sensation swept over Martina.

This might have been *really* happening. She might in reality have been standing here as Hugh's bride, her hand clasped in his, while he claimed her in the same vibrant and emotional tone.

How much was he really feeling? Suddenly she would very much have liked to know.

Somehow the old priest managed to complete the ceremony, although his voice stumbled over Martina's name and once he actually found it difficult to remember Hugh's.

During the confusion they changed places once more, so that Harriet was standing beside Hugh when the priest finally declared,

"*Forasmuch as Hugh and Harriet have consented together in holy wedlock – I pronounce that they be man and wife.*"

Now it was time for the signing of the register. Martina's name would be inscribed, but signed by Harriet.

At last it was all over.

They moved out of the Chapel and into one of the finest rooms in the house where there was breakfast for everyone.

The priest, however, announced that he had another ceremony to perform in the next village, made his apologies and departed.

It was then that the two girls lifted their veils.

While they were processing into the other room, Hugh had stopped to speak to his secretary who assured him that the priest had become so bewildered by the two women looking exactly alike, that it was impossible for anyone to say that a marriage had actually taken place.

"Please write out your report in full," Hugh told him, "and send it to the Bishop with my deepest apologies for this event occurring in my Chapel."

"How are you going to explain to the Bishop that you allowed it to happen?" Martina enquired.

He stared at her.

"I beg your pardon?"

"What will you say if anyone asks why you didn't put a stop to it at the time?"

"I was hoping that *you* could tell me that," he said. "After all, this is your plan. I am merely following your instructions. This is no time to be telling me that they have a flaw."

"But I cannot think of everything," she protested. "I thought that being a man and so much more intelligent than a mere woman, you would know the answer."

Hugh ground his teeth.

"Very well, how about this? I didn't stop it happening because I was drunk. I had been carousing at my stag night and could barely stand up at the altar. You had to hold me up, or Harriet held me up – well, one of you did – or maybe both of you."

"In that case I was mad to marry you," Martina announced with spirit.

"There is certainly somebody mad around here," he told her bluntly, "but it isn't you. Anyway, there it is. I was too drunk to know what was happening."

"How dare you get drunk the night before our wedding!" she pouted indignantly.

"Welcome to married life, Lady Faversham. This is how husbands and wives live. Men get drunk. Women put up with it."

"Not this woman. And you cannot tell the Bishop you were drunk – "

"If you are going to be a nagging wife I shall toss you in the river," he threatened. "At any rate the Bishop will not ask me any questions because we will be far away before he finds out."

He turned back to his secretary.

"When you write to the Bishop, say that as I was so stupid as to allow the wedding ceremony to become a muddle, I enclose a cheque for one hundred pounds as a donation. I hope he will be kind enough to assure me that I am, in fact, not married to anyone."

"He will have to agree," the secretary replied. "There was such confusion that I think there was one moment when the two ladies said part of the responses to each other rather than to the bridegroom."

Hugh actually roared with laughter.

As soon as they had finished breakfast he declared,

"Now the sooner we sail away the better. When you have changed out of those wedding dresses we will be off. Your luggage is already loaded onto my coach, and my own suitcases went on ahead last night, together with a maid from my staff who will look after you on the boat."

"How clever of you to think of everything," Martina enthused. "I shall forgive you for being intoxicated on your great day!"

"Thank you, *madam!*" he said ironically.

Within a short space of time they were aboard one of Sir Hugh's large carriages drawn by four beautiful black horses.

He stood outside while they seated themselves and then asked,

"Are you quite ready, Lady Faversham?"

There was a stunned silence, during which Harriet and Martina looked at each other.

"When you say Lady Faversham," Martina queried delicately, "may I ask which one of us you are addressing?"

He grinned.

"Does it matter?"

"I suppose it doesn't," she agreed. "I am perfectly ready and eager to be gone. What about you, Lady Faversham?"

She inclined her head graciously towards Harriet, who inclined hers back, saying,

"I too am ready, Lady Faversham."

Martina looked at Hugh.

"We are both ready, husband."

Hugh's lips twitched at this performance.

"In that case, my ladies, let us depart without further ado."

He signalled to the coachman, climbed in and settled himself beside Harriet and facing Martina. Then they were off.

"You are now free," Martina cried, seizing her friend's hands.

"Can it really be true?" Harriet wondered. "They must have discovered by now that I have gone. Mama will have read my letter. But what will my stepfather do?"

"He will huff and puff all morning," Hugh ventured, "and then he will read the letter that I sent him, informing him that I have married Miss Shepton and that Miss Lawson is accompanying us on our wedding trip."

"You mean that the other way around," Martina pointed out.

"Do I? Are you sure?"

"I am not sure of anything any more," she admitted.

"Well, it scarcely matters now," he said easily.

"You told him?" Harriet asked, wide-eyed.

"Naturally. What did you expect?"

"Well – " Harriet made a helpless gesture.

"The 'marriage' cannot do you any good if nobody knows about it," Sir Hugh pointed out gently.

"Oh – yes, indeed."

Hugh's eyes met Martina's in a moment of shared humour as Harriet's wits caught up with the situation.

"I also took the liberty of inserting a notice in *The Times* for tomorrow," he added. "I do hope that you will not think that I was taking too much for granted."

"Oh, no, no!" Harriet said. "Whatever you think appropriate."

"You are too kind, madam. I predict that you will be the perfect wife."

"Oh, but – "

"Ignore him," Martina advised. "He's making fun of us. Nobody is married to anybody."

"I am not so sure about that," Hugh intervened wickedly. "I am still single, but I wouldn't take a wager against the chance of you two being married to *each other*!"

They laughed and the atmosphere became more relaxed.

"You can make fun of us if you like," Martina pointed out. "We are both so grateful to you. You have transformed the world almost as if you had waved a magic wand. I want to say thank you, thank you a thousand times."

"Don't thank me," he replied genially. I am going to enjoy this trip with my two charming wives – er – friends. No, don't glare at me. You have just said that I am entitled to my little joke."

"And I expect we are going to hear a lot of that little joke," Martina remarked eyeing him.

"Well, now and then. It is just the exhilaration of finding myself a newly married man, although I must confess I have been slightly disappointed in you two so far."

"Why, whatever do you mean?" Harriet asked.

"He means something disgraceful," Martina said, her eyes kindling. "Take no notice."

"Oh, but I would not like to be remiss in my attention to a gentleman who has done so much for me," Harriet responded. "Pray sir, what were you expecting?"

"To be covered in kisses, at the very least," he answered outrageously. "I believe that is what a bride and groom normally do as soon as they are alone in the carriage that wafts them away to wedded bliss."

"Behave yourself, sir," Martina murmured.

But Harriet took it seriously.

"I did not realise – " she began hesitantly.

"Take no heed of anything he says," Martina told her firmly. "He does not expect to be kissed – not if he is a wise man."

"But you, madam, have much reason to know that I am not a wise man," he came back softly.

His eyes, meeting hers, offered a challenge. For some reason Martina found herself remembering the suffocating kiss he had forced on her yesterday and the blood rose in her cheeks.

"I think – " Harriet started again.

Sir Hugh looked at her kindly.

"I think," resumed Harriet, shy but determined, "that we have much cause to be glad that you are not a wise man, sir. For a wise man would never have embarked on this masquerade in the first place!"

Hugh broke into a smile.

"Charmingly stated, madam. At last, a lady who appreciates me."

He said these last words with a sly glance at Martina who sat fuming in the opposite corner.

Then Harriet astonished everyone, herself included, by kissing Sir Hugh on the cheek.

"You have been so very kind," she whispered softly. "Hasn't he, Martina?"

"Exceptionally," Martina replied coolly.

"Then aren't you going to kiss me too?" Hugh demanded.

"I see no need."

"Martina!" Harriet exclaimed indignantly. "Fie on you for being so ungrateful!"

"Fie on you again for being so ungrateful!" Hugh echoed.

His eyes were gleaming with fun in a way that delighted Martina and at the same time annoyed her.

Hugh sighed dramatically.

"It is so sad when a man is not properly appreciated by his bride – or, in my case, appreciated by one of them and not the other. What shall we do, my dear?"

He turned to Harriet.

"Shall we stop the carriage and dump her by the wayside?"

Harriet gave a little giggle. Martina ground her teeth.

"Oh, very well."

To Martina's surprise she felt suddenly shy, but she determinedly leaned forward and kissed Hugh on the cheek.

"Thank you, my love," he cooed.

"You are most welcome," she said untruthfully.

"You will observe, by the way, that I address you as 'my love' and Harriet as 'my dear'.

"You don't mind me calling you Harriet, do you?" he

asked her quickly. "In the circumstances I can hardly address you as Miss Shepton. It would give rise to suspicion."

"You are very right, sir," she agreed.

"I think it best to address you differently to avoid confusion," he continued, straight-faced. "In case I – er – forget which of you is which."

Harriet giggled again. She seemed to have a taste for Hugh's sense of humour.

It was a taste Martina did not share. In fact, she thought her 'bridegroom's' enjoyment of the situation most ill-judged.

It dawned on her that Hugh was not the tame pussy cat she had imagined and whom she had so carelessly ordered about.

In fact, she was beginning to realise that she had placed Harriet's fate and her own in the hands of a man about whom she knew absolutely nothing at all.

CHAPTER FIVE

Sir Hugh's coachman drove them as far as Woking Railway Station, where they all boarded the train for Portsmouth. They reached the port at three o'clock in the afternoon.

The place was full of bustling life and both Harriet and Martina gazed entranced at the numerous ships.

Hugh had obviously sent instructions ahead that he was arriving and an official came hurrying up to them as soon as they arrived on the dock. He led the way, while several porters were instructed to carry their luggage.

The moment she saw the yacht Martina realised it was larger and more spectacular than she had expected. She had somehow thought it would be quite small and they would have nowhere to move about when they were aboard.

But what she found was a vessel over two hundred feet long, gleaming white except for a cheerful yellow funnel.

She gasped but said nothing. Hugh noticed her silence and remarked,

"I hoped you would be impressed by my yacht. I have had it for two years and it was designed to my own specifications. I am extremely proud of it and I sincerely hope you will be comfortable."

"It is very much more splendid than I had expected it to be." Martina exclaimed.

"That is because I have been travelling a good deal," Sir Hugh answered. "I found that my old yacht, which I had owned for many years and was very fond of, was too small to carry all I need to take with me when I travel to the East and the West. The sea can be very rough at times."

"I am sure we will be safe in this fine yacht, however rough the sea is," Martina commented.

"I can promise you a comfortable journey, ladies. Now, shall we go on board?"

He led them up the gangway and immediately both girls found themselves immersed in a world of luxury and beauty such as they had never imagined.

The Captain greeted them and then Hugh personally escorted them below.

First they walked to Harriet's cabin which was decorated in yellow and gold. She too gasped with delight and began to explore the rich furnishings.

The maid that Hugh had sent on ahead was already on board, unpacking her bags which had just been delivered from the carriage. She began to show Harriet around, indicating the elegant appointments and the little private bathroom. Harriet was ecstatic.

"Let's leave her to it," Hugh whispered to Martina.

Taking her hand he led her to the next cabin which was the same as Harriet's except that it was decorated in pink, with pink hangings and matching flowers. Like Harriet's it boasted a large and comfortable-looking bed.

Both cabins were not only furnished with all modern comforts, but contained pictures and pieces of furniture which were delightfully a part of Britain's history.

Martina had somehow never thought that Hugh was artistic in any way, but the pictures were magnificent. Most people would have thought them far too good to waste on a yacht.

"It is all so beautiful," she breathed. "Your pictures are wonderful, your curtains and carpets are what one seldom sees anywhere except in a drawing room, and although I have not yet tried the bed, I am quite certain it will be very comfortable."

"Try it," he suggested.

Immediately Martina sat down on the bed and finding it soft and springy she bounced up and down with delight.

"In the past," Hugh explained. "I have been so uncomfortable myself in rough seas and on hard beds that I was determined my beds would be a joy to sleep in."

"I think you have been brilliant in creating such a masterpiece," Martina enthused. "But I am equally sure that you enjoyed every minute of it."

"You are quite right," Hugh replied. "I did enjoy decorating this yacht, although not as much as I have enjoyed the thought of decorating my house."

"Only the thought? Haven't you made a start?"

"Oh, no, I am leaving that to you. No one could make my house more attractive than you!"

Martina drew in her breath.

Then, because she felt embarrassed, she walked towards the porthole and said,

"I think now that we are on board the sooner we put to sea the safer we will be."

"We will be leaving at any moment. After departure I want you to forget everything you have just been through. The three of us are starting a great adventure."

"Yes, of course," she agreed brightly.

But even to herself her voice sounded false and nervous.

He was silent for a moment before saying,

"Are you angry with me because I said I wish you to decorate my house?"

"Not – not angry exactly – "

"I will tell you something else. When I was building this yacht, I was thinking of you."

There was a fervour in his voice that increased her embarrassment.

Then before she could answer, Harriet came rushing into the cabin.

"There's a terrible commotion going on outside," she gasped. "There's a man on the quay yelling your name and trying to make them lower the gangplank again. Of course the Captain refused and the man is now threatening to throw himself into the sea and everyone is shouting and – "

"I had better go and look," Hugh said in alarm.

He raced out of the cabin and up to the top deck with Martina and Harriet hurrying after him.

As Harriet had described a young man was dancing with agitation on the quay below them.

Martina thought he looked familiar but for the moment she could not place him.

"Hugh!" the young man shouted. "For pity's sake, let me on board."

"Good Heavens!" Hugh exclaimed. "It's Robin."

"*Hugh! Let me come on board or I swear I'll dive in and swim after you!*"

"Let the gangway down, Captain," Sir Hugh ordered. He was laughing. "Robin, you young devil! What are you doing here?"

"What do you think? What is always the matter when I come flying to you? Let me on board and I will tell you."

The gangway was being lowered. The young man raced up it, carrying a bag, and two sailors ran down to the quay to collect two more bags that he had left on the dock.

Now Martina recognised him as someone she had seen talking to Hugh at Lady Bellingham's ball.

The young man wrung Hugh's hand.

"Thank goodness I caught you before you left. Please, *please* say you are delighted to see me and that I can come with you."

"But you don't know where I am going," Hugh objected. "It might be somewhere you don't care for."

"Is it out of England?"

"Yes."

"Then it will suit me wonderfully well!"

"But whatever has happened to bring you here?"

"I arrived at your house just after you had left. They told me where you were going and I caught the next train. It was a close run thing. When I saw your gangplank going up, I thought I was finished."

"You make it sound so desperate," Hugh commented, laughing. "But the story can wait. Miss Shepton, Miss Lawson, allow me to present my friend Robin, Lord Brompton. So far he may have done little to recommend himself, but I assure you he is the best of good fellows."

"Your servant, ladies," Lord Brompton said, bowing smartly.

The two ladies inclined their heads politely.

"Robin is a very old and dear friend," Hugh continued. "And, as is the way with old friends, he always turns to me when he finds himself in difficulty. From the manner of his arrival I would guess that he is in more than usually large trouble!"

Robin laughed.

"You are so right, I am in a *terrible* mess."

"Well, my other passengers might say the same thing," Hugh observed. "But from you, I am more accustomed to it."

"But who would expect to find two such beautiful angels, who have obviously just dropped down from Heaven?" Robin sighed.

The girls laughed, delighted with his good looks, his charm and his air of merriment.

"That is a really nice compliment," Martina said. "There are many names we have been called but we prefer being angels to anything else."

"Trust Hugh to find something new and unexpected," Robin answered.

"And we are eternally grateful to him," Harriet broke in fervently.

She spoke as if the words came from the very depths of her heart and Robin gave her a wondering look.

As if Hugh was aware they were walking on dangerous ground, he suggested,

"Now come along! Let us cheer as we move away from the coast."

"Will we be departing soon?" Robin asked anxiously.

"Immediately, my dear fellow."

The gangway had been raised again. The engines were thrumming and after a moment the great white ship began to leave the quay behind. The ribbon of water between them grew wider and wider, something which everyone regarded with satisfaction.

"Now we have escaped," Hugh announced calmly.

He had meant the remark for the girls, but it was Robin who piped up,

"Thank goodness for that!"

Hugh looked at him keenly, but said nothing for the moment.

For the next hour everyone was occupied looking over the rail as the ship moved out to sea.

"Let us hope and pray," Hugh said, "that this trip will make everyone of us happier than we have ever been."

His eyes met Martina's, making her want to look away, but she found that she could not do so. She felt as if he was drawing her closer and closer to him. But this was not what she had intended when she planned the escapade.

Then she wondered exactly what it was she had intended. She was usually so confident and independent, but now she was becoming confused.

"It will soon be time for dinner," Hugh proposed. "Ladies, why don't you return to your cabins to change and I will see you in the dining room in an hour."

Harriet and Martina clambered below excitedly to their cabins where they found that the maid had finished unpacking Harriet's bags and had started on Martina's.

They found that she was called Kitty. She was in her late twenties and before going to work at Faversham Place had been employed as a lady's maid.

"But my old Mistress died," she informed them, "and I had to leave. There are no ladies at Faversham Place, so I've been doing general work. But I've always wanted to look after ladies again. It's what I'm good at."

They soon realised that she spoke no more than the truth, handling their clothes with the air of an expert. Kitty had already decided which dresses they should wear for dinner that night and which jewellery would be the most suitable.

Contented, they placed themselves in her hands.

*

"Now," said Hugh when the two men were alone on deck. "Let us have a talk. Since you set out this morning expecting to find me at home, I imagine you don't have your passport with you."

"My dear fellow, you do me an injustice!" Robin replied in an injured tone. "I *always* carry my passport with me."

"The better to make a quick and sudden escape," Hugh observed. "Of course, I should have guessed."

"Well, I think you should. You know me better than anyone and you have helped me make a few escapes. You're not angry with me, are you? It's too late to turn me away now."

"Not unless I throw you into the sea," Hugh agreed, looking down at the foaming waves below. "I am still trying to decide."

Robin leaned against the rail, grinning and raising his champagne glass in salute. All his life his looks and charm had won him acceptance and he recognised that he was in no danger now.

"As a matter of fact," Hugh admitted. "I am delighted that you have joined us. Although I didn't think of it at the time, having an extra man is exactly what I wanted."

"There now, you see, I knew you needed me and hastened to be of service."

"What are you running away from *now*?"

"I don't see any need for you to say *now* in that particular tone, as though I was always – " he saw his friend's cynical eye on him and coloured. "The fact is I have got myself into a very unpleasant mess."

"Good Heavens! What a surprise!"

"All right, have your laugh."

"I intend to. How has this happened again? I told you

the last time you came to me in trouble that you would have to be more careful."

"Yes, indeed you did," Robin responded. "But you know how hopeless it is with me. I suddenly found myself being forced into marriage with a girl who has been pursuing me for the last three or four months simply because I have a title."

"You don't know that," Hugh observed thoughtfully. "She might love you for yourself alone."

Robin considered for a moment. "Do you think that is at all likely?"

"Not really," Hugh said with a grin. "Not unless she is a lady of unusual forbearance, tolerance, patience – "

"All right, I get your drift. I didn't think so either. Although she did once tell me that I had a wonderful mind."

"That you had a – are you sure you understood her properly?"

"Quite sure."

"Then you were quite right to flee her. She was plainly laying a trap, flattering you with lies."

Robin gave a choke of laughter.

"That's what I thought too. You have always saved me in the past, so naturally I hurried off to find you."

"But why has this suddenly become a major problem? You told me about her only the other night, at the Bellinghams' ball – "

"I never mentioned her."

"I am sure you said that Lady Laura Vanwick – "

"Oh, good grief, not her! This is another girl."

"Another girl, who has been pursuing you at the same time as – well, I will not mention the lady's name again. I suppose I shouldn't have mentioned it the first time."

"You know, that's another thing that's always si
me," Robin confided. "The convention abo tl
mentioning a lady's name. I mean, if you don't s
name, how the devil do you both know who you are t
about?"

"And particularly so in your case," Hugh remai
dryly. "Any discussion about you getting into hot water w
a pretty young lady could apply to half the fema
population!"

"That's very true," said his friend, much struck.

"The trouble with you," Hugh told him severely, "is
that you are attracted by every woman you meet."

"Well, the girl *is* very pretty and I danced with her and
it was actually she who suggested we might spend a few days
at the sea."

"You and she went together?" Hugh demanded,
aghast.

"Not exactly. She has an aunt who lives at Weymouth,
so she went to stay with her and I sort of – turned up. It was
all perfectly respectable."

"Until – ?"

"Her father arrived. She wanted to marry me and he
thought it was an excellent idea. In fact he sent me a note to
say that he was coming to see me 'to discuss the future'.
Well, I knew what that meant, so I fled. To you, as always.

"I remember the time when my father was going to
punish me for eating some apples he was going to show at
the County Fair, you saved me from a beating and you have
been saving me ever since."

Hugh laughed.

"That is true," he agreed. "I have never known anyone
get into more trouble than you have managed to do."

"Well, I admit I do find girls very attractive," Robin

ghed. "Unfortunately, they always have parents who are on
e hunt for titles. Which rather spoils what could otherwise
e a beautiful relationship.

"Thank goodness for you, Hugh! Otherwise I would
have been married half-a-dozen times by now. At least, I
don't mean that exactly, since it isn't possible to be married
to more than one woman at a time – did you say something?"

"Not at all," Hugh replied, choking slightly. "Do go on
with your story."

Luckily Robin was too preoccupied with his own
sentiments to notice any oddness in his host's manner.

"Mind you, the last one was a real beauty," he mused.

"The last one? You mean the one with the aunt?"

"No, the last one before her and Laura – Angelica. I
almost – but no! I heard that she managed to marry an
American millionaire, but they quarrelled so violently on the
ship out to New York, that by the time they arrived they were
both asking for a divorce.

"But I have learnt my lesson," Robin continued. "In
the future I am going to be very, very careful. When I do
marry it will be for ever and you will be the Godfather to my
children."

"Don't hurry," Hugh advised. "Once you are married
you are tied down and there is no chance of having an
affaire-de-coeur."

Robin nodded.

"That is just what puts me off the thought of marriage,
it is so very limiting. But I must say I think your two ladies
are very lovely. But two of them! You lucky dog!"

"Behave yourself," Hugh adjured him mildly. "I want
you to be kind and considerate to my guests and not fly away
leaving them in tears with broken hearts."

Robin held up both hands.

"I promise, I promise," he insisted. "It only happened once and you must admit that she was very pretty. But I had no idea until she was with me what a terrible bore she could be."

Hugh regarded his young friend wryly. He was fond of Robin, but he was certainly not blind to his feckless ways. He flitted from girl to girl, falling in and out of love easily, assuming that they would recover as quickly as he did himself.

It would have been too much to call him heartless, but he was certainly thoughtless. Hugh sometimes thought it would do him good to fall seriously in love and experience the pain of loss.

But he did not say any of this. It would have been useless. Only experience would teach him, so he contented himself with remarking,

"When you do marry, for Heaven's sake let me approve of your bride, or I will doubtless have her crying on my shoulder or else threatening to kill you and having to take the gun from her hand.

"Or maybe even," he added reflectively, "failing to take the gun from her hand. Now, why don't we dress for dinner and join the ladies?"

*

As the weather was warm dinner was served on deck.

The ladies emerged from below, Harriet wearing a soft yellow dress of tulle and satin with a pearl necklace about her throat.

Martina was dressed more strikingly in deep blue adorned with sapphires. Hugh took her by the hand and led her to the table, leaving Robin to attend to Harriet.

The meal was as delicious as could be found in any London restaurant. Hugh's chef had been warned that only the best would do on this journey and he had outdone himself.

"And now, do tell us where we are going," Martina enquired.

"Tonight we shall put in at Cherbourg. My chef needs to buy some French cheeses, so I think we might have a day ashore."

"But after that," she begged.

"After that is a secret."

"All the best journeys are a secret," Robin intervened enthusiastically. "Here's to the unknown!"

He raised his glass and Harriet did the same so that they clinked.

While the table was being cleared for the next course, Martina wandered to the rail and stood gazing out over the water where the sun had already set and darkness was gathering. After a moment Hugh came and joined her.

"You always said that you would like to take me to sea," she said. "Can't you tell me now where we are going?"

"No, if I don't tell you, you cannot refuse to go."

"Of course I will not refuse. How could I when you have been so kind?

"Praise indeed!" he said. "But you have always looked down your nose at me in the past and run away when I have tried to tell you what I wanted. You cannot run away from me now."

That was true, Martina reflected. And again she had the feeling that this Hugh was a man she did not know.

"I think I ran away because you frightened me," she replied. "Now I may have to jump into the sea and swim home."

"I think you would find that very difficult," Hugh parried. "But I have always found you get what you want, regardless of who tries to stop you."

"That sounds horrid," Martina protested. "If I have wanted something, it is because I have wanted to help someone and not because I wanted it for myself."

There was silence for a moment.

Then Hugh said,

"I think you are wonderful. The more I see of you, the more I want to see. The more I talk to you the more I want to hear what you have to tell me. Now one of my dreams has come true. You are actually here with me in the middle of the ocean."

"And one of my dreams too," she sighed, "since I have always longed to travel."

There was another long silence.

Then Hugh asked her,

"Am I in your dreams?"

Martina turned to look at him and her eyes twinkled.

"Perhaps."

"That is the kindest word you have ever said to me. For the rest, I shall have to bear my soul in patience."

"Time for a toast," Robin called, coming up behind them with Harriet.

They carried champagne glasses and each held one out to the others. When they all held a glass Robin proposed,

"Here's to travelling into unknown waters and finding adventure wherever we arrive.

"Amen to that!" exclaimed Hugh.

"And so say I," Martina added.

"And I," Harriet echoed.

"And I as well," Robin finished.

Then they were all laughing. Laughing until it seemed to Martina as if the sea itself was laughing with them.

CHAPTER SIX

Soon they could see the lights of Cherbourg and an hour later they were gliding into port.

Leaning over the rail eagerly watching the sailors at work, Harriet gave a huge yawn and was immediately horrified at herself.

"I am so sorry!" she apologised.

"We were up very early this morning," Martina reminded her. "I am quite sleepy myself. But I simply must have a glimpse of Cherbourg first."

She walked to the rail but almost at once she too was yawning.

"Go to bed, both of you," Hugh commanded. "We will spend the night here and tomorrow we can explore Cherbourg for three hours. My chef says it will take him at least that time to buy all he needs in the market. I suggest we all retire."

Later, safe in her cabin, Harriet knelt down to say her prayers, thanking God for saving her from the horrors which had been waiting for her at home.

She could imagine how furious her stepfather would be when he found that she had disappeared. She could only pray that he would not catch up with them, but she feared that he might try to do so.

'He will be furious that I have brought so much of my

money with me,' she thought.

At the same time she was sure that now she was with Hugh and Martina they would protect her however aggressive and violent her stepfather became.

'And Lord Brompton,' she whispered. 'For I am sure that he too would protect me.'

On that happy thought she climbed into bed and soon fell fast asleep.

She dreamt that she was a child again and her mother was holding her in her arms.

In the next cabin Martina as well was snuggled down in the most comfortable bed she had ever slept in.

And now that the drama of the day was over she was suffering a reaction. When she thought of the risks they had taken and how easily everything might have gone wrong, she was almost faint with relief.

'We were so lucky,' she pondered, 'that Hugh has been so understanding and so kind. And so clever, I must admit. It might have been otherwise. What a risk I took throwing us on the mercy of a man I do not really know.

'And the truth is, I actually don't know him *at all,* although I used to think I did. I am not sure why, but I once considered him rather dull.

'Nobody but he would have agreed to this incredible idea. But did he do it for me or because he enjoys challenges that are unusual and adventurous?'

She reminded herself that since they had boarded his yacht he was still hinting about how much she meant to him. Surely that proved he had done it for her?

But somehow she was not quite convinced. And she wanted to be.

'I suppose it is because he is different from anyone else I have ever met,' she thought, 'I could not see what a marvellous man he really is. I have been very silly in refusing even to listen to him when he proposed.'

She smiled to herself.

'Well, there is still time yet. We are all going to learn so much about each other before this journey is over.'

She fell asleep feeling happy.

The following morning they slept late and nobody troubled them.

Martina was to learn afterwards that the Steward had been given strict instructions never to wake any of the guests, but to let them sleep on for as long as they pleased.

"You must always remember," Sir Hugh had told his crew, "that most people go to sea when they are either overworked or worried and upset personally.

"You are therefore to pander to them and to make them forget everything but the fact that they are enjoying themselves, and that there is nothing to upset or frighten them on board. I want them to forget whatever might have happened in the past."

His crew thought it a strange order. But they soon learnt that when their Master travelled he was usually accompanied by a friend who was suffering in some unusual way.

There were gentlemen who had lost all their money and who were on the verge of committing suicide.

There were ladies who had lost their husbands, a child or a lover and wanted only to cry on the Master's shoulder until, in some magical way, he made them smile and see that life could still be worth living.

Sir Hugh had chosen each man who worked on board his yacht not only because he knew his job but because of his character. He must have a nature that Sir Hugh personally found congenial. As a result the atmosphere on the ship was gentle and kindly.

Both girls felt it when they awoke the next day to the gleaming light from beyond the porthole. Kitty looked in on each of them and said they were to be served breakfast in their cabins while they dressed, and the gentlemen would be waiting for them when they were ready.

An hour later they advanced on deck, Harriet in an elegant walking dress of dark blue and Martina attired in olive green.

Together the four of them left the yacht and took a carriage to explore Cherbourg.

They did not head for any particular place. It was enough to have escaped and be free to roam as they wished.

They enjoyed lunch at an outdoor restaurant, raising sparkling glasses to the sun and watching the light wink off them.

A spirit of mischief impelled Martina to comment,

"Your arrival is delightful, Lord Brompton – "

"Robin, please," he said at once.

"Very well. Your arrival is delightful, Robin, since it makes us an even number – "

"That is just what I said," Hugh declared at once.

"But would it be tactless to enquire as to what we owe this pleasure?" Martina quizzed.

"Yes, it might," Hugh said.

"You mean," Robin answered, "what terrible crime did I commit that made it necessary for me to run away?"

"Yes, that was exactly what I meant," Martina said without hesitation.

Hugh covered his eyes. Harriet looked mildly shocked at this forwardness.

"Of course," she hastened to say, "it doesn't really concern us – "

"Nonsense, of course it does," Martina interrupted. "After all, we are *all* refugees."

"Whatever from?" Robin asked.

"That need not concern you," Hugh intervened with a small frown at Martina and Harriet.

That frown said, '*Robin in a charming boy, but he is not sufficiently reliable to be entrusted with our story.*'

The quick-witted young man took in everything.

"Now why am I being excluded from your great secret?" he wanted to know.

"Because you are an addle-pated young fool," Hugh told him bluntly. "And a gentleman does not enquire into a lady's secrets – so be silent!

"For myself," he continued, "there is no secret in my flight. I am fleeing boredom."

"You can never get bored with me around," Robin said at once.

"That I believe," Hugh agreed fervently and they all laughed.

"I must confess," Robin muttered in a penitent voice that fooled nobody sitting at the table in the sun, "that I have been extremely wicked – "

"How thrilling!" Martina cried.

"He hasn't been wicked at all," Hugh said in a dampening voice, "just a complete and utter fool, as usual."

"You see how it is," Robin replied mournfully. "My friend, Hugh, knows me better than anyone. I always turn to him to rescue me from the result of my folly. Then I go back and start all over again."

They laughed even louder but Harriet said softly,

"I am sure you are not as bad as you paint yourself."

Robin was laughing, but he stopped and turned

towards her. As he looked at her, a gentle smile came over his face.

"Nobody could be as bad as I paint myself," he concurred. "Thank you so much for your understanding. Perhaps now I can believe in myself again."

When they walked on after lunch, they seemed to divide naturally into two parties with Martina and Hugh in front, the other two dawdling behind, engrossed in conversation.

"I am not really sure I approve of your friend," Martina murmured. "His way of implying that he is a bad character is very clever. It makes one think that he is modest and self-critical, which I suspect is the reverse of the truth."

"Is any man ever truly modest?" he asked.

"A good point. But I also suspect him to be devoted only to his own pleasure and a cunning schemer."

There was a thunderstruck silence before Hugh exclaimed in a stunned voice,

"Martina, if we are to talk about *scheming* – "

"That is quite a different matter," she said hastily.

He grinned. "I am glad you think so."

"Shall we walk on?" she suggested primly.

It might have been accidental that Robin did not walk too quickly or he might simply have been considerate to Harriet, who was clinging to his arm. For one reason or another they fell behind.

"Are you beginning to feel better yet?" he asked kindly.

"I – I don't quite know what you mean?" she stammered, on her guard. She too had understood the significance of Hugh's frown, and although Robin charmed her she was not yet sure that he was a solid character.

"Hugh's guests are usually suffering in some way and

he brings them for a trip on his yacht to help them. I just wondered why you were unhappy."

"How do you know the problem is mine?" Harriet hedged. "Perhaps it is Martina who needs help, and I am simply here as her chaperone?"

"Perhaps, but I see a sadness in your eyes that makes me wonder. I think you have been very frightened. I see you look out over the sea, almost as though you were afraid of being pursued."

"Oh, yes, I am," she burst out. "I am running away from my stepfather who wants to marry me to the most terrible man, a huge, red-faced, bawling vulgar creature called Brendan Muncaster."

"Good grief!" Robin exclaimed. *"Him!"*

"You know him?"

"I met him once at the Bellinghams' ball the other night. I saw you and Miss Lawson there too, although we were not introduced. I cannot believe that any lady would want to ally herself to an object like Muncaster."

"He would carry me away to the North, where nobody would ever see me again," Harriet said. "What could I do but run away?"

"Nothing," Robin replied fervently. "Of course you had to flee."

"I was so lucky that Martina helped me. I was in despair, but she thought of the cleverest plan – " Harriet broke off suddenly.

"You mean she thought of appealing to Hugh?" he asked.

"Yes," Harriet agreed hurriedly. "That's what I meant. "We fled to his house and – and he saved us."

"By bringing both of you abroad on his yacht?" Robin encouraged her.

"Yes, that is what he did."

Robin waited to see if she would say any more, but it was plain he was not going to learn any secrets from her.

He shrugged good-humouredly. He could wait. His eyes were fixed on her face and the movements of her pretty mouth.

Harriet was devoutly thankful that he asked her no more questions. She knew that she was not as quick-witted as Martina, who would have dealt with him easily.

Besides, she did not feel like a duel of wits with Robin. She merely desired to walk in the summer sun with him, occasionally glancing into his handsome, kindly face and feeling happy.

At last the two couples joined up again and returned to the ship.

The chef arrived just ahead of them with a carriage full of vegetables, meats, cheeses and spices.

"Good Heavens, we must be going on a very long voyage," Martina exclaimed in a significant voice.

"I suppose we must," Hugh said, with a twinkle in his eyes. "Why, what is it?"

His question was in response to a gasp from Harriet, who was staring out to sea.

"What's that?" she demanded, indicating a ship that was advancing quickly.

"The mail boat from England," Hugh told her.

"Does it take passengers?"

"Sometimes."

"Oh, please," she begged, "will we be leaving soon?"

"Almost at once," he assured her. "Let's go aboard."

They did so and Harriet went straight to the rail, watching the approaching boat with frightened eyes.

"You think your stepfather would pursue you across the water?" Robin asked, coming up beside her.

"I don't know," she whispered in terror, "but to me every man on that deck looks like him."

"Well, if one of them *is* him, he had better not see you here," Robin suggested. "Look away."

She obeyed him and somehow her face ended up against his coat and his arms moved protectively around her.

"Do not worry," he murmured. "I won't let anything happen to you."

*

Martina chose the gown she meant to wear for the evening and took it to Harriet's room. It made it easier for Kitty to dress them together, and it gave her the chance to keep a protective eye on Harriet.

For herself she had chosen a dress of dark blue silk trimmed with lace and set off by sapphires. Kitty dressed her fair hair into an elaborate creation. She looked magnificent.

Harriet was not magnificent, but she was pretty and charming in her soft yellow gown adorned with pearls. She looked what she was, a gentle, unassuming girl with a sweet retiring nature.

The gentlemen were waiting for them in the dining room on the next deck. They were both elegantly dressed in white tie and tails.

Martina thought that she had never seen Hugh look so handsome.

"We are not eating outside tonight," he told Martina. "I think Harriet will feel more at ease if she is safely under cover, although I promise you there is no boat in pursuit."

"Thank you, that's most understanding," Martina said with a smile.

"Am I allowed to tell you that you look splendid

tonight? My other wife is also pretty, of course – "

"Hush, you must not talk like that in front of Robin. I think you were quite right not to tell him."

"So do I. A more feather-brained young idiot I never did meet. But it's a pity in a way. I was enjoying the joke!"

"What you were enjoying," she told him severely, "was the prospect of being covered in kisses by two young women."

"No, only one," he parried quietly.

His remark left her at a loss for words. Suddenly her heart was beating faster and she was wondering why she had never realised how dangerously attractive this man was, and how much more interesting than mere boys.

Robin for all his pretty face and charming ways aroused in her nothing but indifference.

As they were about to head for the dining room, Robin moved alongside Martina and murmured,

"Is Miss Shepton all right? She seemed so distressed this afternoon."

"She is much recovered now, thank you."

"I had no idea that she had suffered so much. How brave she is! We must all take great care of her."

"We *are* taking great care of her, Lord Brompton," Martina replied with a touch of irony in her voice.

To Hugh, a few minutes later, she observed crossly,

"That young man can be rather annoying. I do not need him to tell me to take care of my friend."

"Be kind to him. He's falling in love."

"Again?"

"What do you know about that?"

"When a young man flees as he has done, he is usually running away from a trip up the aisle!"

"That is certainly most perceptive of you. I had not realised you were such an astute judge of the world. Another feather in your cap."

"Actually I cheated," Martina confessed ruefully. "I am not being astute. I heard people talking about him at the Bellinghams' ball!"

Hugh roared with laughter.

"I should have known you would keep a trick or two up your sleeve," he said appreciatively.

"I couldn't place him at first, but in the last half hour it has come back to me. He is known as a hardened flirt. I think I should warn Harriet about him."

"By all means, if you want her to find him more attractive than ever."

She sighed.

"You are right. There is nothing like a bad reputation to enhance a man in a woman's eyes."

"I wish I had known you felt like that, I would have had several desperate affairs and made as much scandal as possible."

"But then you would not have been you," she replied. "And I would have hated that."

He took her hand smiling.

"Let us go inside before I say something extremely foolish."

"Why not say it?"

"Because you have always reproved my foolishness in the past."

"I don't think I would mind you being just a little bit foolish."

He regarded her with his head on one side.

"What game are you playing, Martina? I mistrust that demure tone."

Their eyes met. Each was regarding the other with faint humour, spiced with curiosity.

Anything might happen now – anything at all –

"I say, come along you two," Robin called. "We're feeling hungry."

Hugh gave a little sigh and his lips shaped the words, "another time."

"Yes," Martina murmured.

"We are coming," he responded, taking her hand.

They ate at a small round table, seating themselves so that the two ladies faced each other and the two gentlemen likewise. This made it possible for Harriet and Robin to plunge into conversion, leaving Martina and Hugh to talk together.

"You still haven't told me where we are going," she reminded him.

"Ultimately the Mediterranean. We are sailing South down the coast of Spain, through the Straits of Gibraltar and then on to Monte Carlo."

"Monte Carlo!" she breathed in delight.

"You once told me that you longed to see it."

"And you remembered?"

"I remember everything you have ever told me about yourself," he replied lightly. "Mind you, I did once plan to take you there on our honeymoon – "

"Well, in a way, that is just what you *are* doing," she murmured.

"I do not think you should have said that, madam. It was most improper."

"Well, really! Many people would say this whole expedition is improper."

"Does that worry you?" he enquired, regarding her curiously.

"Not in the least."

"Well done! I always admire your spirit. May I pour you some more wine?"

"Just a little more, thank you."

"And you, Miss Shepton? Miss Shepton?"

He had to raise his voice a little before Harriet heard him, so engrossed was she in what Robin was saying. She accepted some wine and so did he, but then they returned to being absorbed in each other.

To her surprise and delight, Harriet had realised that Robin, despite his light-hearted manner, had an interest in flowers and birds that equalled her own.

She had never met this before in any young gentleman. Usually they shared her interest in horses, but the majority of men thought flowers and birds were a female delight and they were too masculine to profess any particular interest in them.

But Robin liked both and had learnt a great deal about them from his mother, whose garden was famous.

He too was reacting with delight at finding a woman who was content for him to discuss flowers and birds rather than pay her compliments.

"What I have always wanted," Harriet said, "is a huge garden sloping down to a stream. I long to feel, when I am moving amongst the flowers that this is a Heaven of its own and the flowers themselves want me to love them."

"I know exactly how you feel," Robin agreed. "But I have always found that when I was in the company of a woman she wanted me to talk about her and not about her surroundings."

"Oh, yes, people grow bored at discussing such topics," Harriet pointed out eagerly. "They either want to be praised or gossip unpleasantly about their friends."

"You should see my mother's garden. "She has taken so much trouble in finding new flowers. Some of them come from abroad. Those by the stream have come from strange rivers she has visited in different parts of the world."

Harriet clasped her hands together and pleaded,

"Oh, you must let me see them. I so long to find the garden I have dreamt of, but now I am afraid of going home."

"When we do go home I will look after you," Robin promised.

"That may not be for some time," Martina observed in a discouraging voice.

"However long it takes, I shall be waiting," Robin declared fervently, his eyes still riveted on Harriet.

"You ought to put a stop to this," Martina muttered to Hugh. "He is only amusing himself."

"I am not sure that he is," Hugh whispered. "In any case, putting a stop to it would be quite beyond my power."

Neither of the other two had noticed this exchange.

"You can come to my family's country house," Robin was saying. "My mother would love to meet you and we will give you a false name for safety."

"Whatever would you call me?"

"I was just thinking while we were talking, which flower you remind me of," he replied. "I decided it was one particular one and maybe you will be a little disappointed that it is not more exotic.

"It is one of the flowers I love the best, especially as it appears when the winter is over and the spring has just arrived."

"I cannot think which flower you mean."

"I was thinking that you remind me of a primrose, especially as you look now," he added, with a glance at her dress. They are such pretty gentle flowers."

"I think that is beautiful and I am very happy to be a primrose," Harriet breathed.

"I am so glad because to me a primrose means the beauty and delight of spring. It means the sunshine and, more important than anything else, the happiness which comes with love and is true and real and not pretending to be anything different."

"I know what you mean and thank you for being so complimentary. But I am afraid that perhaps now I will never be able to see the soft gentleness of the English spring again."

"You are not to be frightened," Robin urged. "You have me to look after you now."

Harriet gave him her gentle smile.

"When you talk like that, I am not afraid."

"What we have to do," he said, "is make every moment count. It is always a great mistake to look into the future. None of us really knows what will happen. Our destiny may lie somewhere very different from where we are at the moment. So forget yesterday and think only of tomorrow."

Harriet smiled at him.

"Oh, yes," she agreed, "and I am trying to do just that. It is so wonderful to be here and to be able to talk to you without being afraid of what I may say."

"I want you to say exactly what you feel in your heart," he replied seriously. "And I shall do the same."

They smiled at each other. Then somehow there was no need to say any more.

CHAPTER SEVEN

After dinner Robin took Harriet for a stroll on deck under the stars leaving the other two behind.

"Did you hear their conversation?" Martina exclaimed, exasperated.

"I heard" replied Hugh, "but I am sure I don't know what there was to annoy you."

"If you believe that young man loves flowers you will believe anything," she declared. She imitated Robin mockingly. 'Come and see my mother's garden and I adore primroses.' Honestly!"

Hugh grinned.

"Unlikely as it sounds, it's all true. His mother does have a wonderful garden. And since he is devoted to his mother he has really learned a great deal from her. He knows plants and loves them. I promise you there is more to Robin than the rather shallow young man he may seem at first."

"Indeed? Well, you know him much better than I, so I shall trust your judgement," she said demurely.

He eyed her with misgiving.

"Come, Martina, this meekness is most unlike you. Trusting my judgement? Whatever are you thinking about?"

"There is no need to cast aspersions on my character."

"I was not. I admire you. The trouble is that you are

normally so positive and determined that when you say anything meek and docile it does not sound like you."

"I can be as meek and docile as any woman," she informed him. "And if you dare to disagree I'll tread on your foot!"

"That's my girl!" he applauded appreciatively.

They laughed together.

"Seriously," she said, "can that rattle-pate be trusted up on deck with Harriet in the moonlight?"

"Perhaps we had better go and act like chaperones."

They climbed up the steps and strolled along the deck listening to the sound of the water. Above them the moon was briefly hidden by clouds, but suddenly it emerged, flooding the scene below with silver light and causing Hugh to stop suddenly.

"Look," he whispered.

The moonlight had picked out the figures of two young people embracing, oblivious to the entire world.

"This is terrible!" Martina cried. "You must stop them."

"Why? I never tell my guests what to do. Neither of us has any authority in this matter. And it was *you* who said she might meet somebody on this journey."

"But I didn't mean – "

"Nobody can choose for someone else, Martina. We all love where we love. Sometimes we wish we didn't, but it happens whether we want it or not."

She guessed what he was really saying to her, and her heart leapt.

"Let us creep away," Hugh mumbled. "We are not needed here."

Laughing they retreated and soon the moon had vanished again, so that she could barely see him leaning on the rail and regarding her.

The sight of Harriet with Robin had affected Martina. Now she recalled again the moment when Hugh had pulled her into his arms and kissed her with fierce passion, so much at variance with his normal gentlemanly self.

He too must be thinking of that moment, she was sure, thinking about it and longing to repeat it.

Just as she was longing for him to kiss her again, if she was to be honest with herself.

She looked at Hugh trying to tell him without words that she needed his kiss.

Instead he took her hand and held it between both his. After a moment, with her pulses racing as she wondered what he meant to do, he dropped his head and laid his lips against the back of her hand.

Then, without raising his head, he turned her hand over and kissed her palm with lips that seemed to scorch her. Pleasure travelled like wildfire up her arm and across her skin until she was trembling with delight.

Martina took deep breaths to steady herself against the power of such strong feelings. Surely now he would kiss her, as she yearned for him to do.

But he looked up at her. When he spoke it was in an unsteady voice.

"Forgive me," he said. "I gave you my word."

"Wh-what?"

"That day you came to my house and I – behaved disgracefully, you made me promise never to repeat it. You made it clear that you could not entrust yourself to me unless I gave you my word as a gentleman."

This was not how Martina remembered the incident at all. It was true that Hugh had promised not to kiss her again, but she was quite unable to recall having demanded it.

In fact, she would have had to be losing her senses to ask him for any such promise.

And, far from losing her senses, she had the feeling of having only just come to them.

"I pledged my word to you that I would not behave in such a way again," he repeated.

She pulled herself together.

"It is perfectly all right, Hugh. Please do not concern yourself."

"You are very kind. Perhaps you should retire below now before I forget myself again."

She could have screamed with frustration.

'*Go on, forget yourself*!' she wanted to cry. '*Stop being a gentleman and kiss me!*'

Instead, she merely inclined her head graciously and slipped her arm through his. He walked her to the steps that led below and watched until she was out of sight.

Martina almost ran to her cabin. She was pervaded with a sense of adventure, a *new* kind of adventure.

It was going to be hard to flirt with Hugh, she realised. She had rejected him so often in the past that now he no longer knew what to make of her.

But that made him a challenge and even more interesting.

Martina's eyes gleamed in anticipation of the duel to come.

*

When they met the next morning, Martina greeted Hugh with a demure smile and a polite hope that he had spent a restful night.

Hugh courteously thanked her for her enquiry, but mourned the fact that his night had been troubled.

"For some reason I simply could not go to sleep," he sighed. "My thoughts disturbed me, madam."

"Any particular thoughts?"

"The usual ones – with perhaps a few new variations."

Her lips twitched.

"My sympathies, sir."

"Your pity is wasted, madam. I enjoyed my thoughts and dreams immensely." His eyes gleamed. "As I always do."

"I am so delighted to hear it."

"May I ask if you enjoyed a restful night?"

"Perfectly, thank you. I fell asleep as soon as my head touched the pillow. As I always do."

"You are very fortunate. *Robin, Harriet,* how nice to see you this morning. I trust you spent an enjoyable evening after you left us."

"Thank you, it was most interesting," Robin responded solemnly.

"Lord Brompton was showing me the stars," Harriet sighed, "and explaining all the different constellations."

"That must have been most enlightening," Hugh agreed.

His eye flickered briefly towards Martina, sharing the knowledge of what they had both seen the night before. She laid her hand over her mouth to hide her giggles.

From then on everything was subtly changed.

Without a word being said, they each knew that she was no longer indifferent to him but that the situation was far from simple.

Hugh was a proud man, prouder than Martina had ever imagined. He had offered himself to her and been rejected more than once. Now he was cautious, unwilling to admit his love too freely to a woman who might merely be indulging a caprice.

One thing was beyond doubt. This man was not going to fall at her feet and thank her for finally noticing him. And she found that she respected him more for that.

"How long before we reach Monte Carlo?" she asked later that day as they stood gazing out to sea.

"I am not quite certain that Monte Carlo is an entirely proper place for a young lady to be so eager to visit," he replied in a censorious voice. "Nice might be better, or Menton."

"I believe they have recently opened a train from Nice to Menton," Martina observed. "And it passes through Monte Carlo."

"Meaning that if I stop in either of those places you will jump ship and catch the next train?"

"Meaning precisely that."

"Fie, Miss Lawson. Anyone would think you cared for gambling."

"Perhaps I do. How can I tell until I have visited a casino?"

It was fifteen years since the lavish, extravagant casino had been opened in Monte Carlo. Now that there was also a new railway and a main road, visitors flocked there, attracted by the glittering high life.

Luxurious hotels had sprung up. The Grand Theatre had been opened with a special performance by the great actress Sarah Bernhardt. Monte Carlo was *the* place to be.

"I must confess that I am surprised at you," Hugh admonished her, "and a little disappointed."

"Why?"

"I understood that you were devoted to Reason."

"I am."

"Monte Carlo is known for many pleasures, but few of them, I believe, are intellectual."

"I did not say I was intellectual, I merely pointed out that I was devoted to Reason," she crowed triumphantly. "I am sure, if I think hard enough that I can work out a *reason* for enjoying Monte Carlo."

He grinned.

"That is your own personal kind of logic, is it? You invented it?"

"If we are going to talk about logic, I think you will come off rather badly, Hugh. I remember certain remarks of yours about how women should not possess too many brains. I have now decided that you are right. Henceforth I shall live a life of frivolity!"

"That I should like to see."

"You will see it," she prophesied.

"I doubt it. Frivolity does not come naturally to you. But I own I should like to see you being more light-hearted."

Martina gave a little sigh.

"One day – when I know that Harriet is safe."

"Cannot you forget your responsibilities for one moment and think of yourself?"

"But I certainly will when we reach Monte Carlo. And in case you think I am going to reduce you to bankruptcy, have no fear. I have brought my own money and so has Harriet.

"In fact, we both wish to pay our own way and perhaps it's time you and I spoke about this issue. Neither of us wishes to be a charge on you."

"Good grief, Martina!" he cried, revolted. "Do you think that I would expect you to pay for your keep? Is that your opinion of me?"

"Well, is it your opinion of me that I will simply

impose on you without thought of the cost?"

"I thought we were friends. You know I don't care what it costs."

"Yes, but – please, Hugh, don't be offended."

"Should I not be offended when you offer me money? Excuse me!"

Without another word he walked away, leaving her alone and dismayed.

At one time she would have thought she could predict exactly what Hugh would say or do in any situation. Now his reactions took her by surprise. Clearly his pride had been offended and she supposed she ought to have realised that it might be.

She wandered along the deck to the sun lounge and sat there, comfortably shielded from the wind, watching the ocean slip past. It was here that Hugh found her a few minutes later.

He was followed into the lounge by a Steward bearing coffee and cakes, which he set down on a low table. When the Steward had left Hugh said,

"Am I forgiven? I really did not mean to be so ill-tempered."

"I didn't mean to be so clumsy. It was just that I dumped myself and Harriet onto you, without asking you if – well – "

"If I could afford it?" he teased.

"You know that's not what I meant. I just felt a little awkward."

"With such an old friend, you should not have done. Now, let's forget all about it. And keep your money to lose at the tables."

Martina considered for a moment and then decided to risk a small lure.

"Why do you bother with me?" she enquired.

"I ask myself that all the time. 'Why do I bother with her?' I muse in the small hours. 'Why don't I just toss her overboard? It would be so easy. No one would miss her.'"

She smiled her appreciation at his tactics.

"And what answer do you give yourself?" she asked.

"I don't. It is a mystery beyond comprehension why anyone should bother with you for one moment. I may come to a decision one day, but by that time we will probably both be old and grey."

"I wonder what we will be doing when we are old and grey," she pondered.

"I wonder too."

The door of the saloon opened and Harriet looked in, smiling when she saw them.

"Is Robin not with you?" Hugh asked as she came over and sat with them.

"No, he's on the bridge, trying to persuade the Captain to let him take the wheel."

"Good Heavens!" Hugh muttered faintly.

"Don't worry, the Captain was standing firm," Harriet reassured him. "He said even if he would have considered it normally, which he wouldn't, it was out of the question when we were about to pass through the Straits of Gibraltar, because it is only eight miles wide."

"Perfectly true," Hugh said with relief.

"I am afraid Robin didn't appreciate it. He said eight miles was plenty of room."

"Some people could run a ship aground in eighty miles. Thank goodness my Captain has a sense of duty."

"I have been asking Hugh when we will reach Monte Carlo," Martina piped up.

"Some time tomorrow according to the Captain," Harriet said. "Probably in the evening."

"I thought we would put into Gibraltar tonight," Hugh remarked, adding innocently, "unless, of course, you ladies would prefer to go in the other direction and stop in Tangier."

"You are going to say something outrageous, aren't you?" Martina asked in a resigned voice. "Why should we prefer Tangier?"

"I just thought it might be an easier place for a man with two wives to find acceptance!"

He finished with a glint of mischief in his eyes that both girls found irresistible. They burst out laughing and Hugh, sitting between them, put an arm around each of their shoulders and laughed with them.

"That's all very well," Martina said, "but you might find it awkward to decide who is wife number one and who is wife number two."

"Not at all," he responded calmly. "I shall let you fight over me and award myself to the victor."

They all chuckled again and then looked up to see that Robin had just entered the saloon.

"I say, Hugh, that Captain of yours won't let me pilot the ship into Gibraltar."

"Shame on him! Did you explain how brilliant you are in a rowing boat?"

"Yes, but the scurvy fellow was not impressed!"

*

They had almost reached the port of Gibraltar. The yacht, already travelling slowly, slowed even more and began the tricky entrance, while they crowded on deck and watched in admiration as the Captain glided in.

"Well, I suppose he did manage better than I would have done," Robin admitted to the amusement of the others.

They went ashore and found a restaurant for lunch, then split up into two parties for an afternoon of sight-seeing.

It was quite clear that Harriet and Robin were determined to be alone together and Martina was deeply content wandering the streets on Hugh's arm.

"You are not really reconciled to them making a match of it, are you?" he asked.

"Oh, I am becoming resigned to it. I don't dislike him, but I wanted somebody more solid and dependable for Harriet."

"But is that what she wants for herself. He is a bit of a silly fellow, but I think she finds it endearing, much as his mother would. Some women are made that way."

"Yes," Martina agreed in a wondering voice. "Harriet is like that. I didn't see it. Very well, I give my consent reluctantly, because as you say he is a silly fellow and you couldn't always rely on him to stick exactly to the facts."

"I am sure Harriet will appreciate his weakness and will refrain from questioning him too closely in their married life."

She gave a little shudder.

"What sort of a married life would that turn out to be?"

"I believe they will be very happy."

"Well, it would not do for me – a man you could not trust to tell the truth about absolutely everything."

"Be fair Martina. Nobody tells the truth about absolutely everything."

"You do," she said at once. "Do you know, I realise now that the reason I turned to you so confidently was because I knew by instinct that you are the most honest man alive and I could trust you absolutely. And you have proved me right!"

"Yes, but – we all have our secrets. Do you mean you

could not trust me if you knew that I had kept something to myself?"

"Oh, I don't mean that. Of course we all have secrets, but I know that you would never *deceive* me. You would never tell me that you were doing one thing and then do another. It just isn't in you. I know that."

"And if you found that you were wrong," he asked slowly, "that would be the end?"

"Of course. I would mind more with you than with anyone else, because I trust you more than anyone else. But I have no fear. After all, I put my fate into your hands, didn't I?"

He took her hand in his. He seemed both moved and confused.

"I do not deserve such trust," he mumbled huskily. "No man deserves it. I am afraid that one day you will discover that and blame me."

"I am not afraid," she answered softly.

"Martina, if only I – if you only understood – "

"Perhaps I do," she said tenderly.

"There is something I have longed to say to you – "

"Is it really so hard?" she asked.

Her pulses were racing. The moment was here. He was going to ask her to marry him once more and this time there was no doubt as to what her answer would be.

"You have no idea how hard it is," he admitted. "After what you have just said to me – "

She laughed at him.

"Oh, my dear! Just because I have told you I admire and respect you more than any other man I know, why should that dismay you as it seems to?"

"Because it is such a great burden and responsibility," he replied gravely.

"Isn't it one that you have placed on *me*, whenever you have asked me to marry you?" she quizzed him, "and whenever you have said that you love me?"

"And you feel that my love is a burden," he sighed.

"No, that is not what I am saying," she told him eagerly. "I am saying that you can say anything to me that you want."

Why did he take so long? she wondered. Had she not given him enough hints, even reminding him of previous proposals?

"You think it's so easy," he said. "But you make me afraid."

"Afraid?"

"Afraid to fail you. Afraid of your judgement when I do fail. I think – "

"Yes?"

"I think I have now realised that I am a coward and that maybe it is better to hope and to dream."

She frowned and there was a little ache of disappointment in her heart.

"I do not understand you," she said at last.

"Perhaps neither of us has understood each other very well. This voyage has already been one of discovery in many ways."

"Hugh – "

"Do not look alarmed, my dear. I think my wits are wandering and I am talking nonsense. It is a beautiful day and tomorrow we will be in Monte Carlo. Let's banish serious thoughts and concentrate only on enjoying ourselves."

From then on he put himself out to be charming and light-hearted in a way that would once have delighted her.

But now Martina was aware of a faint uneasiness at the

back of her mind. Their relationship had seemed to be going so well, yet in the last few minutes there had been a false step, either on his part or on hers. She was not even sure which. All she knew for sure was that something was wrong.

At last she managed to put such thoughts aside and enjoy herself as Hugh had urged.

They met up again with Harriet and Robin and ate dinner in a little restaurant by the waterfront.

Then it was time to stroll back to the ship, hanging on Hugh's arm and laughing at his jokes.

She could not recall him ever being so merry.

They bade each other goodnight and retired to their cabins.

Martina slept well and when she awoke in the morning it was to find that the ship had left Gibraltar at first light and they were on their way to Monte Carlo.

CHAPTER EIGHT

They made good time to the little Principality of Monaco arriving in the late afternoon on the next day. Martina's first view was the sun gleaming on the marvellous pink palace, built high on a cliff overlooking the harbour.

The town of Monte Carlo rose steeply and behind it the hills reared even higher. She took a long breath of happy expectation.

They had already eaten on board and were now ready to disembark. Hugh took their passports to the Harbour Master's Office and returned with all kinds of useful information.

"There is a concert at the Grand Theatre tonight," he announced, "and it is strongly rumoured that the Prince will be present."

Everyone agreed that they wanted to see His Serene Highness Prince Charles III, who had ruled Monaco for thirty-four years.

But Martina did add,

"Will there be time to go to the casino afterwards?"

"No," Hugh said firmly. "Wait until the following night when you can give it all your energy. Not to mention all your money."

"That's what you think, but I am going to win. You wait and see."

"I will wait with bated breath. Now if you ladies will hurry and dress, it will soon be time to leave."

A carriage was waiting for them on the quay an hour later. The two gentlemen were splendid in evening dress. Harriet wore her pale yellow gown, her 'primrose' dress as she now called it and was rewarded by seeing Robin's eyes light up.

Martina's dress was ivory satin adorned with diamonds on her wrists and about her neck. On her head she wore a diamond tiara and diamond ear rings hung from her ears.

She too had the satisfaction of seeing Hugh's eyes gleam at the sight of her. He took her hand and carried it to his lips before handing her gallantly into the carriage.

Martina's first sight of the Grand Theatre struck her dumb with wonder. Although small it was an extravagant fantasy of cherubs, tassels, scrolls, luxurious drapes and gilt, gilt everywhere.

At the back in the centre was the Prince's box, another symphony in gilt and tassels. As she entered the stalls on Hugh's arm, Martina gazed up, seeing that the box was empty for the moment.

She was not rewarded until the last moment. Just before the lights faded, an elderly man with a thick grey beard, walked very slowly into the box and stood stiffly to attention, flanked by courtiers as the National Anthem was played.

The performance was a concert of operatic pieces, mostly light-hearted with some love duets.

The last item before the interval was a duet from Mozart's *Don Giovanni*. As the Don made advances to Zerlina she struggled to decide about him, singing, *"Vorrei, e non vorrei ?* I want to say yes and yet I don't want to."

Nothing could better express Martina's own

confusion, except that gradually she was becoming convinced that she did want to say *yes*.

Suddenly she had a conviction that Hugh was watching her. Turning her head slowly she found that indeed his eyes were fixed on her and there was a look of understanding in them. He too had recognised her in the music.

She smiled back at him, feeling a comfortable sense that they belonged together because he could read her mind.

It was not as exciting as being kissed, but it carried a sweetness that was very pleasant.

During the interval they drank coffee and discussed the evening. Harriet was thrilled with her surroundings. After the restricted social life forced on her by her stepfather, she felt as though she had gone to Heaven.

"And to think I actually saw the Prince," she breathed.

"Yes, he is very impressive," Hugh said, "but you have to feel sorry for the poor fellow. He is almost completely blind. He has been that way for years."

"How sad!" Harriet exclaimed. "Why, that reminds me of – oh, dear! I feel rather guilty now."

"Why ever should you feel guilty?" Robin asked curiously.

"Well, doesn't it make you feel guilty?" Martina put in quickly. "Here we are enjoying ourselves and never thinking of how the world has been spoiled for him. I wonder what it's like to hear a concert but be unable to see anything."

"It must be very tragic for him," Robin replied and the conversation passed on to other matters.

Martina breathed a sigh of relief. Harriet had been thinking of the half-blind elderly priest at the wedding ceremony, forgetting that Robin knew nothing about their scheme.

When the performance was over and the audience was streaming out into the warm night, Hugh said,

"I think it would suit me to walk back to the yacht. It isn't a long walk. Miss Lawson, would you care to join me?"

"Yes, I too would enjoy the walk," Martina agreed at once.

Robin and Harriet promptly declared that they would prefer the carriage and a few moments later they were bowling away down the road to the harbour.

"I wonder why they didn't choose to walk with us?" Martina asked mischievously.

"Because they were not going to lose the chance of a *tête-à-tête*," he replied, adding with a grin, "neither was I."

"For shame, sir. I thought you truly wanted to take some healthy exercise."

"You thought nothing of the kind. You knew I wanted to be alone with you."

"You misjudge me. I am not vain enough to think that I might figure in your calculations."

She almost skipped along the road ahead of him glancing back over her shoulder laughing.

At the bottom of the sloping road they could see the harbour filled with brilliantly lit boats. High overhead the stars wheeled in the velvety night.

Suddenly Martina felt happy and confident, sure that her power over Hugh was as strong as ever and it only needed a little time to bring matters to a happy conclusion.

"You have never been vain," he said, also laughing and following her.

"Come now, have you never felt that I have too good an opinion of myself?"

"Tact and discretion will keep me silent on that score," he riposted.

He caught up with her and drew her arm through his.

"But you were right about my calculations," Hugh continued. "It's in my nature to plan things. It always has been. I am not spontaneous, like Robin."

"None the worse for that. Robin speaks and acts first and thinks later, if at all."

"Well, I cannot deny it, but his heart is warm. He will be an affectionate husband."

"I think you are going a little too fast."

"I understood that you had given your consent."

"I am resigned, but I think she could do better."

"Brendan Muncaster?"

"That isn't fair!"

"I think it is. Robin has an old and honourable title and is immensely rich. What's more he loves her and so she can be the making of him. Some men are like that, you know. They are naturally malleable and a good wife can influence such a husband as she pleases."

"Malleable?" she mused. "Nobody could call you malleable."

"No, I am proud and stubborn. I decide what I want and I don't turn back until I get it, even when the wanting is unreasonable. A good friend once told me that I have a head of granite."

They were walking side by side now, her arm through his. An open carriage passed them. The passengers were a young man and a girl, locked in an embrace. They were not kissing but staring into each other's faces, oblivious to the entire world.

Suddenly the night seemed to be full of couples walking hand in hand, embracing in the shadows.

In Monte Carlo the very air seemed to be alive with romance, and Martina, who had thought herself devoted to

111

Reason, began to appreciate that there were other more thrilling horizons to explore.

"I do believe that your head is made of granite," she said. "But what of your heart?"

"Don't you think you know all there is to be known about my heart?"

"Oh, no," Martina replied seriously. "Nobody knows about anyone else's heart."

"What a wise woman you have become. It's not so long since you told me that you would settle for a cold and lonely life, as long as it was interesting. How my heart quailed at the suggestion that I bored you."

"I said a lot of things I shouldn't have said, because in those days – I didn't understand – "

"Understand what?" Hugh asked as she hesitated.

"Things that – perhaps – I have come to understand since. I didn't mean to be unkind when I said that. I just didn't think. I was not wise in those days, not in the special way that I am now."

Now she had given him a chance. He would ask about the 'special way' she had become wise and she could hint at her love for him and he would ask her to marry him.

But the silence stretched on and on and still he did not speak. A chill began to creep over her heart and when she looked at him his eyes were fixed on the ground.

"Well," he said at long last and it seemed to Martina that he spoke heavily, "there is much to be said for obtaining wisdom. Nobody can be the worse for it."

"Unless wisdom teaches you a lesson that you do not wish to learn," she fenced.

"How true. I know that I am not the man I was. I have learned – much against my will – to mistrust my own instincts."

The chill spread out from her heart to encompass her whole body. He was telling her that he no longer loved her.

"I told you that I am a man who likes to plan well ahead," he continued, as though he had not felt the slight tightening of her hand on his arm. "I try to look forward and see the pitfalls and work out how to avoid them."

"Hugh, what are you saying?"

He seemed not to hear her.

"And then I find that while I was complimenting myself on my cleverness, I created another pitfall that I never foresaw. And when I did uncover it, it was too late and I am deep in trouble and there is no way out."

She stopped in front of him and placed her hands on his shoulders.

"You are now talking in riddles, Hugh."

He looked down at her face and smiled gently,

"Yes, I am, aren't I?"

"Will you not tell me what you mean?"

"My dear, I cannot – not just yet. Not until I see my way clear."

"You are frightening me. It has always been so simple between us."

He gave a half laugh.

"Yes, very simple. I am saying *please* and you are saying *no*."

"I did not mean that. I only meant that it's different now. Those days are over. I wouldn't want to go back to them."

"Neither would I," he agreed at once. "But things have happened that I cannot tell you about – yet."

"But – one day?"

"One day. And when that happens – well, I can only

hope that you will understand. In the meantime, we will continue to be – as we were. But you will know that I hold you in my heart. And I always will."

She gave a sigh of relief.

"I was afraid that you no longer loved me."

"I shall love you all my life. Nothing could make me stop loving you. Nothing. Do you understand?"

"Oh, yes," she sighed gladly. "And I love you too, Hugh."

"Hush! Do not say it too soon."

"I am not. But I know it now."

"My dear," he said huskily. "*My darling*!"

They were at a bend in the road and on the words he drew her into the shadows, tightening his arms about her and covering her mouth with his own.

She responded with her whole heart. She was still confused about Hugh. She knew there was something going on in his head that she did not comprehend. But now his lips were on hers.

Feelings mattered. Hearts mattered. Her heart was all his and at this very moment she could believe that his heart was all hers.

She pressed closer to him, seeking to tell him within the limits of modesty that she loved him in every possible way – heart, soul and body.

When he drew back she could feel that he was trembling. Even his voice shook as he said,

"We must return – to the boat quickly. It is not proper – for me to keep you out here alone."

"Not proper?" she whispered.

"Highly improper."

She knew what he meant. At this moment she too felt

improper. And, what was more shocking, she was loving it.

Hugh drew her hand through his arm again and they continued their walk down to the harbour, strolling side by side, in step, looking very proper.

Martina wondered what passers-by would think if they knew how her emotions were raging behind her sedate exterior.

But all the passers-by were in love as well. And nobody gave them a glance.

*

They spent the next day exploring the Principality, returning in the afternoon to prepare for the evening.

They dined at the *Hotel de Paris*.

Martina was in a state of excitement. She could not discern where this sudden yearning to gamble had come from, but she was looking forward intensely to the coming evening.

She knew she looked at her best in a gown of deep pink set off by pearls. Harriet also wore pearls but with a white gown. Now and then she turned her head close to Robin's, whispering secrets, her eyes shining.

"I trust you have brought plenty of money with you?" Hugh said to Martina, smiling at her excitement.

"I have all my money with me," she declared.

"Well, for Heaven's sake be discreet about it, at least while you still have it."

"I shall keep it and when we go home I shall have doubled it. Trebled it!"

"Where *is* the sensible girl I used to know?"

"She grew weary of being sensible," she riposted at once. "You have been deceived by me all this while. Beware!"

He laughed.

"I am content to take my chances."

They toasted each other in champagne and set off to the casino in high spirits.

From the *Hotel de Paris* it was a short walk across the gardens to the elaborately decorated casino with its two towers and fluttering flags. As they climbed up the broad steps to the triple entrance, liveried doormen bowed and ushered them inside.

The famous casino was just as Martina had hoped, as lavishly gilded as a theatre with huge glittering chandeliers hanging low over the gaming tables.

Already the crowd had built up. Lavishly dressed ladies in silks, satins and gorgeous jewels were escorted by gentlemen in white tie and tails.

Some of them wandered from table to table, watching the others play with idle interest. Others sat at tables, regarding the spin of the wheel with hard intense eyes.

The wheel stopped, the croupier called the number and someone would smile broadly, while the others looked as though their hearts had sunk.

Robin was talking to Harriet in a low voice, telling her all about the various forms of gambling.

"In which he is an expert," Hugh murmured in Martina's ear.

"I expect you are an expert too," she muttered back.

"I have played a game or two in my time," he replied, realising too late where she was leading him.

"Good, then you can tell me what to do."

"That depends on what you want to play. They seem to cater for all tastes here."

"Let's start with the roulette wheel," she suggested.

"Well, I don't need to tell you how that works. You put

your money on and you lose it. In an hour you won't hav[e] penny left and you will then have to marry me for m[y] money!"

"Or I will win millions of francs," she challenged.

"In that case, *I* will marry you for *your* money."

"Oh, no! If I make millions I will want a Duke at least."

He grinned.

"Miss Lawson, you are incorrigible. Come along, let's buy you some chips."

Armed with a small fortune in chips she took her seat at a table with a roulette wheel, watched the play for a moment and then made her first stake.

At first it seemed as though Hugh might be right.

She lost and lost again.

Glancing up, expecting to see severity in his face, she found only a wry humour.

Perhaps, she thought, he really was content to see her lose all her money and be forced to marry him.

But then she reconsidered. What there was between them was too beautiful for that.

Next she began to win.

She staked on black thirteen and the ball fell into the slot. She staked on red twenty and the ball fell into the slot.

Excitement gripped her. The room faded. Her companions faded, all except one. There was only herself, Hugh and the roulette table.

When she won she staked everything on the next spin. And the next.

"That's enough," Hugh whispered. "You have now won quite as much money as I would demand for a dowry."

"Oh, hush!" she told him. "Just one more. That's all I want."

By now the news had spread around the room and people were crowding in from the other tables.

Everyone stared as Martina piled all her chips onto black fifteen.

The wheel spun. The ball danced and fell.

Black fifteen.

A cheer went up around the table for her success gave all the gamblers heart.

The croupier pushed a mountain of chips towards her.

"That's it," Hugh declared.

"Yes, I do think so," she agreed.

Her crazy mood had vanished as quickly as it had begun.

Hugh came with her as she cashed in her chips.

"Now let's leave before I have a nervous collapse," he said.

They made a triumphant procession out of the casino. Several people tried to touch Martina to see if her luck would rub off.

An open carriage was waiting outside to take them away. Hugh handed Martina in, but kept tight hold of her when they were all seated.

"I am afraid you will fly away," he explained.

"I think I might," she agreed. "I feel as light as air."

"Martina, how could you take such a risk?" Harriet asked in awe.

"I loved it," she said. "I suppose I am naturally reckless."

"The sooner we leave Monte Carlo, the better," Hugh announced.

"Oh, but I want to come back tomorrow," Martina pleaded.

"Definitely not. You could never have another evening like this. You would lose it all."

"Who cares?" she asked magnificently.

Standing up in the carriage she threw her arms up to the sky and cried,

"I won. *I won!*"

"So much for being devoted to Reason," Hugh commented, firmly making her sit down. "A babe in arms would be more reasonable than you at this moment."

She answered him with a mischievous smile. She was quite content to leave his arm firmly around her.

He did not remove it until they were safely aboard the boat.

"I have a good mind to tell the Captain to leave at first light," he declared.

"Don't do that," Robin piped up quickly. "We haven't explored the neighbourhood yet. I thought we might take the train to Nice."

"Very well, we will stay just a little longer, but we are *not* going back to the casino."

"Anyone would think you didn't trust me," Martina teased.

"And they would be right." He placed his hands on her shoulder. "Goodnight, my dear. Enjoy your victory, but don't think of trying to repeat it."

"No, I have a much better victory in mind," she said, giving him a significant look. "Goodnight."

She took Harriet's hand and they walked away together. The two men watched until they were out of sight.

"I think I'll turn in as well," Hugh said. "Tonight's excitement has worn me out."

*

Robin nodded and made his way to his cabin. But once inside he did not prepare for bed, but paced about restlessly. The evening's events had left him exhilarated. The sight of a big win, even if not his own, had been a joyous experience. Now his blood was on fire. Surely now he too must be lucky?

He knew the casino would still be open and there was time for him to put in a couple of hours at the tables. He considered inviting Hugh to go with him, but decided against. Hugh would only disapprove.

He slipped out of his cabin and climbed quietly up on deck. He could see Hugh standing by the rail, but luckily he was gazing out to sea. Robin managed to slip down the gangway unobserved.

It took him only a few moments to hail a passing cab and travel the short distance to the casino. As he had hoped it was still open, the lights blazing merrily out onto the street.

Robin almost danced inside and strode straight to one of the tables.

For a while luck teased him.

First he lost and then he won. Then he lost heavily. Staking all on one throw of the dice he managed to win it all back again. Now he had neither gained nor lost and he felt dispirited.

He rose from the table and walked glumly around trying to decide what to do next,

"Brompton! I say, Brompton, old fellow!"

Robin looked up in answer to the voice that had called him and his face brightened.

"Parker!" he yelled cheerfully. "By all that's amazing! Fancy meeting you here!"

The two old school friends pummelled each other vigorously about the shoulders, uttering cries of satisfaction at their unexpected meeting.

In fact they were far from being as close as their greeting might have suggested. True they had shared a classroom, but the Honourable Jimmy Parker would not normally have been Robin's chosen companion in adulthood.

He was well-intentioned, even kindly, but he possessed a loud voice and a vulgar mind that always led him to put the crudest interpretation on anyone's behaviour.

He was rich enough to care for no man's opinion and no woman's either. He was generous with money, always ready to treat the whole party, but too willing to believe that money explained everything.

Tonight though, Robin was in the mood to feel that a couple of hours of Jimmy's convivial company was just what he needed.

"Let's find a place where we can crack open a bottle and have a good talk," Jimmy suggested.

"You sound as though you have cracked a few bottles already," Robin observed mildly.

The Honourable Jimmy roared with laughter at this brilliant witticism.

They made their way to the saloon, ordered a bottle of port and sat back to enjoy it.

"By Jove, this is marvellous!" said Jimmy. "Everyone was wondering what became of you when you just vanished. Of course we all knew why."

"Not a word about that," Robin put in hastily.

"All right. No names. But the lady wasted no time grieving over you. I hear she has a Duke in her sights now."

"I wish her the very best of luck".

"So do I! Mind you, I wish the Duke even better luck, *hey, hey, hey, hey*!"

121

He finished with a hyena laugh that made the people nearby flinch.

"They were taking bets in the clubs about where you had gone," he carried on. "You weren't in any of your usual haunts. You had vanished right off the face of the earth!"

"I imagine you might have guessed where. Who do I always go to when I need help?"

"Sir Hugh Faversham," Jimmy responded. "So we thought – until we learned that he was on his honeymoon."

Robin set down his glass sharply.

"*What?*"

"My dear fellow, he would hardly take you along when he wanted to be alone with his bride. Or do I mean brides?"

He gave a bellow of laughter at his own wit, while Robin stared at him with an uncomfortable feeling that the hairs were standing up on the back of his neck.

"What the devil are you talking about, Jimmy?"

"I am talking about Sir Hugh and this very strange marriage – or marriages – he seems to have contracted. But since you left the country at about the same time, I suppose you might not know."

Robin signalled a passing waiter and ordered a decanter of whisky. He was beginning to feel badly in need of it.

When the whisky arrived he poured one for Jimmy and a large one for himself, which he drained quickly.

"Now," he began, "tell me everything."

CHAPTER NINE

Fortified by whisky and the eager interest of his audience, Jimmy settled in for a comfortable gossip.

"Well, the first anyone knew about all this was an announcement in *The Times*. 'The marriage is announced between Sir Hugh Faversham and Miss Martina Lawson. The nuptial celebrations were quiet and had been held quickly in view of Sir Hugh's urgent need to travel abroad'."

Robin relaxed slightly as his worst fears were allayed. But he was puzzled by the story. Hugh and Martina had made no mention of a marriage, neither were they behaving like a bridal couple.

"Anyway, that's the least of it," Jimmy continued. "Sir Hugh's secretary has been telling some strange stories about a double wedding."

"*What?*" Robin asked sharply. "You mean there was another couple?"

"Not another couple, my dear fellow. Another bride. Two brides, one groom, if you get my meaning."

Robin merely stared at him. He was beginning to feel sick.

"The secretary was not supposed to talk about it, of course, but apparently he got very drunk and said a good deal more than he should have done. There were apparently *two* ladies at the wedding."

"There's nothing strange in that," Robin commented in a voice that sounded odd to his own ears. "Most brides are accompanied by an attendant."

"Yes, but how many bridal attendants wear a white veil identical to the bride's?"

"What – do you mean?"

"I tell you, neither of their faces could be seen. The secretary swears that they took it in turns to make the responses and by the time they were finished nobody knew which one he'd married. Could be both for all I know, *hey, hey, hey, hey!*"

"That's a damned unfunny joke," Robin growled hoarsely.

"But it's no joke. It is fact. Plain as I am sitting here. What's more the announcement in *The Times* said that the bride and groom had left for the Continent on their honeymoon, accompanied by Miss Harriet Shepton."

He waited for his friend's reply, but Robin could only regard him with a haunted expression on his face.

"Isn't that the most incredible tale you've ever heard?" Jimmy demanded. "Sir Hugh's a wily old dog if you ask me. He couldn't make up his mind between the two ladies, so he's contrived to marry them both!"

Robin hailed the waiter who, in obedience to his command, brought another decanter of whisky. He poured himself a large glass and tossed it back.

A memory was sniffing round the edges of his consciousness daring him to allow it to enter.

On their first night out at sea, he had been telling Hugh about his flight and remarking that but for his friend he would have been married half-a-dozen times by now.

Then he had checked himself, saying that it wasn't possible to be married to more than one woman at a time.

124

Hugh had made a small sound, half a grunt, half a choke of laughter.

Robin had barely noticed it at the time, but he remembered it ominously now and the hasty way that Hugh had changed the subject.

It meant nothing he tried to reassure himself. But that odd reaction lingered in his mind, making him feel cold all over.

He made a valiant effort to speak normally, even humorously.

"You ought to be careful, Jimmy. A fellow could find himself in trouble spreading stories like this."

"But it's all true, I swear it. The secretary was present at the wedding and afterwards Sir Hugh gave him a letter to the Archbishop of Canterbury, or someone like that, apologising for the mistake and offering a large donation to the Church to have it made all right and tight."

"Just imagine that! Fancy being able to arrange for a second wife."

"I think," Robin said, speaking with difficulty, "that your humour is most ill-judged. To speak of two ladies in such a – such a – "

"Oh, really, old fellow! It's the best tale of the century. I only wish I knew some more about what really went on, because I'll wager it's a deal more scandalous than anyone knows. But I was on the verge of leaving the country myself, so I had to be off."

Robin took another gulp of whisky, thinking that if Jimmy did not shut up soon he would do something desperate.

"You know, they must have planned it very carefully beforehand," Jimmy was reflecting.

"I am quite sure," Robin replied in a choking voice,

"that it was a simple mistake – "

"What, with them both turning up in identical veils in that convenient fashion? And then vanishing immediately afterwards?

"The odd thing is that everyone knows Hugh's been sweet on Miss Lawson for ages. Mind you, the girls are like sisters. The rumour is that Miss Shepton's ghastly stepfather wanted to marry her off to some manufacturer.

"That was probably what made her do it. Faced with a choice of marrying the factory owner, or joining a sweet little *ménage a trois,* she chose the *ménage.* You cannot blame Hugh. If a fellow can get two for the price of one, why not, *hey, hey, hey, hey, hey?*"

He ended with violent honks of laughter that made his listener flinch.

"And Miss Lawson?" Robin asked in an icy voice. "Was she supposed to make no objection to having a third party in her marriage?"

"I have told you, those girls are thick as thieves."

"Just the same – "

"Look, I'll let you into a secret, old boy. Females aren't like us. No really, they aren't.

"They're not raised to stand by principles of duty and honour like we are. They are practical. They make the best of things and Hugh's rolling in money. He can probably afford to stay abroad for a long time and who's to know the difference?

"I dare say they will all settle in one of those Eastern countries where nobody will mind about his harem!"

The next moment the Honourable Jimmy was lying on his back on the floor covered in whisky. Robin had knocked him flat before storming out of the casino.

Afterwards Robin had only the vaguest idea of how he

managed to return to the yacht. At first he headed his steps away from the harbour, but after an hour he turned back and walked without noticing where he was going. Somehow he reached his destination and climbed up the gangway without mishap.

As he undressed for bed he found that the walk had calmed him. Perhaps it was the effect of breathing in cool, clean air after the smoky atmosphere of the casino, but now he could see Jimmy's ramblings for the nonsense they were.

'How could I have taken such drivel seriously, even for a moment?' he thought, managing to smile at himself. In this more cheerful mood, he fell asleep.

But he awoke sharply an hour later, sitting up in bed, overtaken by a memory of something that had seemed innocent at the time, but now froze his blood.

On the day that they passed through the Straits of Gibraltar he had spent some time on the bridge with the Captain and then gone in search of Harriet, whom he had found in the saloon with Martina and Hugh.

Looking through the saloon windows he had seen Hugh, sitting between the two girls with an arm around each of them, while they all laughed together.

He could see that Martina was speaking. Through the glass he could not hear what she said, but as he pushed open the door he caught her final words."

" – *wife number two.*"

No, it was nonsense, he tried to tell himself now. She could not have said that. It was an hallucination born of his disordered brain.

But then he remembered Hugh speaking, less clearly than Martina, so that only a few words had reached him.

"– *fight over me.*"

And the three of them had laughed together again.

At the hideous possibilities raised by his memories of that snippet of conversation, sweat stood out on Robin's brow and he jumped up from his bed.

He went back out on deck and stood gazing up at the stars, which had once seemed so romantic to him. Now they only seemed to swing coldly overhead, unyielding, almost threatening.

*

Robin was first into the breakfast room next day, desperate to see Harriet's face and read from it whatever he could.

The first expression he saw was one of sweet concern.

"Dearest, are you ill?" she asked, laying a hand on his arm. "You are so pale and you look as if you haven't slept a wink."

"It's true, I slept very badly," he told her.

Already her manner was bringing relief. This darling girl, whose whole attention was for him, could never be the cynical harlot of Jimmy's story. It had all been a bad dream.

"We all slept very badly," Hugh added, arriving in the saloon just in time to catch the conversation. "I am haunted by the thought of all that cash on board. It kept me awake all night."

As if to prove it, he yawned, just as Martina entered.

"I was awake all night too," she joined in. "Gloating."

"For the last time, will you allow me to lock all that money in the safe?" he demanded.

"For the last time, *no*," she replied firmly.

He glared. She glared back. Although no openly hostile words were spoken, the atmosphere between them remained fraught for the rest of the day.

At the railway station they caught the train to Nice where they did some sight-seeing.

Nobody really enjoyed the expedition. Martina and Hugh were annoyed with each other. Robin was troubled by his thoughts and Harriet was unhappy because of the atmosphere she could detect amongst the others.

They spent the afternoon strolling around an art gallery. The ladies ambled ahead while the two gentlemen fell back talking.

Robin was mentally struggling over various ways to start what he wanted to say. '*I say Hugh, I met an old friend and guess what he's saying about you –* '

But that did not sound quite right.

Somehow the talk turned to Robin's reasons for fleeing England.

"You will have to worry about match-making until the day you marry," Hugh observed.

"I am not the only one who has suffered from match-making Mamas," Robin parried. "You must have attracted your own share."

"And I am very good at fending them off," Hugh said firmly.

There was a brief silence during which Robin struggled with himself. He had told himself that he must be strong and dismiss Jimmy's lurid stories.

But after a tense moment he could not stop himself saying,

"Isn't it time you thought of getting married yourself, Hugh? After all, you will need a son to carry on your title."

"I would never marry for such a reason," Hugh answered quietly. "It has to be the right woman or none at all."

"But how can you tell if a woman is the right one?" Robin asked, trying to sound casual, although sweat was standing out on his forehead.

"If your heart doesn't tell you, nothing else will," Hugh replied. "And if I cannot marry the right wife, I would rather be left with no wife at all."

This should have been reassuring, but in Robin's tortured mood everything he heard sounded ominous.

They were mostly silent on the way home. Everyone was tired and by common consent they dined aboard the ship.

When the meal was over Robin climbed out on-deck to smoke a cigar. Harriet briefly considered following him, but decided against it. His uncertain mood was beginning to make her feel nervous.

After a while she came out with Hugh and Martina and they leaned on the rail, looking up at the Palace on the hill.

"The Captain tells me that there is to be a presentation at the Palace tomorrow," Hugh said. "I could always put our names down and we could attend."

Martina gave a little choke of laughter. Her mood had improved.

"I do not think that would be a very good idea," she replied. "Imagine how it would sound when we are announced. Sir Hugh Faversham, Lady Faversham and Lady Faversham!"

Hugh gave a delighted chuckle and Harriet too joined in the merriment.

"*No!*"

The wail of agony from the shadows made them all turn. Robin was standing there, his face deadly pale and distraught, his eyes wild.

"So it *is* true," he cried, stepping closer. "I would not believe it when he told me. But the whole ghastly thing *is* true."

"Who told you what?" Hugh demanded.

"Jimmy Parker!"

"Good grief, if you are going to believe anything that clown says – when did you talk to him?"

"Last night. I returned alone to the casino. And I did not believe it when he told me that you had married two girls in the same service. But it's true, isn't it? *Two Lady Favershams.*"

"Now look – " Hugh began.

"I have heard you joking about it and not understood because I trusted you."

"And so you can – " Hugh tried to say.

"Can I? Can you look me in the eye and tell me that there was no wedding ceremony?"

"There was, but – "

"With two brides?"

"In a sense, but – "

"In a sense." Robin seethed. "That's it, isn't it? It can be any sense you want. How convenient!"

"Robin," Hugh urged sharply, "be careful what you say."

"It was only a way of helping Harriet escape her dreadful stepfather," Martina intervened. "He was trying to force her into a terrible marriage. It had to be a sham wedding with some doubt about which of us Hugh was really marrying."

"Which of you – ?" Robin echoed aghast. He stared at Harriet. "Are you his wife or not?"

"I – I don't know," she stammered. "Nobody knows."

"So it could be either or both? Lady Faversham and Lady Faversham. I believe you were enjoying a joke about it only a few moments ago."

"Robin," Hugh stated firmly. "There is *no* Lady Faversham."

131

"You mean you hope there isn't. You hope the Archbishop will sort it out for you, but suppose he cannot. You will find yourself married to one of them. But which one, eh?"

"If you will allow me to explain – " Hugh began angrily.

"I want none of your explanations," Robin retorted hoarsely. "How could any of you take part in such a shabby charade?"

"Because we had no choice," Martina added sternly. "Who are you to judge? Where were you when we needed help?"

"Who am I to judge?" Robin whispered, his eyes fixed on Harriet. "Harriet do you hear me? I am the man who loves you and who wants to marry you. But how can I marry *Lady Faversham?*"

"You have now said enough," Hugh told him.

"Yes, I have. I have said enough, I have seen enough and I have heard enough. I cannot bear the sight of any of you any longer."

Turning, Robin began to run away from them.

"Robin," Harriet screamed. "Come back. *Please* don't go."

But he was hurrying down the gangway and could not hear her. She burst into tears and Martina gathered her into her arms.

"I am afraid that young man's manners leave a great deal to be desired," Hugh commented angrily.

"Oh, Hugh, please go after him," Harriet begged. "I could not bear him to come to harm."

"He is more likely to get drunk," Hugh fumed.

"*Please!*"

"All right, I will follow and calm him down. Don't

worry, ladies. Everything is going to be all right."

He left them and after a moment they saw him going down the gangway and racing off after Robin into the darkness.

Harriet wept against Martina's shoulder.

"Come along," Martina soothed her. "You heard what he said. It is going to be all right."

"But how can it be? Robin blames me, I know he does."

"Well, he decidedly has no right to," Martina said crisply.

Inwardly she hoped that Hugh would manage to knock some of the nonsense out of Robin before they returned.

"Let's go down to your cabin," she suggested.

Harriet allowed herself to be led away and in a few minutes they entered her cabin. Kitty fetched them some tea and then left them alone.

"You can be sure that Hugh will explain everything to Robin," Martina soothed her, "and he will understand that we had no choice."

"I don't think that will make any difference," Harriet said forlornly. "You heard what he said. He thinks it's shabby. In his eyes he thinks I am – *besmirched*."

She burst into tears again as she uttered the terrible word.

Martina tore her hair.

"Well if he thinks anything so stupid, you are well rid of him," she declared. "I never met a man who annoyed me more."

"But I love him," Harriet wept.

"Then you have windmills in your brain."

"But love is without reason," Harriet cried

passionately. "You have told me so yourself. That's why you used to say that you would never let yourself fall in love. You said Reason was better."

"I once talked a lot of nonsense," Martina ventured, thinking fondly of Hugh. "Besides, I fell in love with a reasonable man, so I have the best of both worlds."

"You *do* love Hugh, don't you?" Harriet queried shyly.

"Oh, yes, of course I do. I cannot imagine why I did not realise it before, but since we have been together on this trip I have seen things about him I never appreciated. Now I cannot imagine how terrible it would be if I could not marry him."

"You mean if he turned out to be married to me?" Harriet asked.

"No fear of that. Don't forget it is *my* name on the marriage certificate. Wait! Why didn't I think of it?

"If we show the certificate to Robin that will at least allay his fears that you might be the one legally married. That is what he is really afraid about, that he might find himself in love with a married woman, as then he would have to go away and not see you again. Where is the certificate?"

"I – I don't know. I am not sure that I have it."

"Didn't the priest give you one?"

"Yes, but I – "

"And we came away immediately afterwards, so you must have packed it in your luggage somewhere. We must look."

"Oh, yes, let's find it and all may still be well."

They began to turn out the drawers, tossing clothes in all directions in their urgency to find the missing certificate.

"Can I help you?" came a voice from the doorway. Kitty had returned.

"We need to find something urgently," Martina told her. "It's a marriage certificate. Miss Shepton brought it on board when she arrived."

"A marriage certificate – ?" Kitty repeated, looking uneasily between them.

"Between Sir Hugh Faversham and Miss Martina Lawson," Harriet said, oblivious to Kitty's startled face.

"Yes, miss," Kitty mumbled faintly.

She got to work and since she was more organised than either of the others, it was she who finally produced a piece of paper from the back of a drawer.

"This looks like it," she crowed triumphantly. But then she glanced at it and her face fell.

"I'm sorry miss, I'm a bit confused. You said Sir Hugh and Miss Lawson, but it says here, Sir Hugh and Miss Shepton."

There was a freezing silence.

"That's impossible," Martina mumbled at last.

With shaking hands she took the certificate. But there was no mistake. The bride's name was given as Harriet Shepton.

Martina sat down because her legs were already giving way beneath her.

This was impossible.

It *had* to be impossible.

Harriet sat beside her and took the certificate in her own trembling hands.

"I don't understand," Martina said. "They wrote the certificate from what it says in the register and you signed *my* name there, so my name should be here."

Harriet gave a little gasp and buried her face in her hands.

"Harriet?" Martina asked urgently. "You were supposed to sign my name."

"I know, I know and I meant to – at least, I thought I had – but everything was so confused and I was so nervous and I just – I think – oh, dear!"

"Oh, dear!" Martina echoed.

"But does it really make any difference?" Harriet asked. "I made the responses in your name when we stood at the altar, so now if it says my name – surely that adds to the confusion?"

"Yes, in a way," Martina said, trying to derive some comfort from this thought. "It's just that – "

It was just that there was something very definite about words on paper that she had not realised until now. The certificate said that Harriet was married to Hugh, so did the register. As for the responses – who was to say who had said what?

When it all came to be sorted out, there was every chance that Harriet would be declared Hugh's wife. The written records said that she was.

Martina's blood ran cold. How could her plan, which had seemed so clever and easy at the time, end like this?

It was just not possible. She could not, *must* not lose him.

But in her heart she knew that the worst was possible and she could feel the pain creeping over her.

"Am I married to Hugh?" Harriet whispered.

"I am afraid you might be," Martina muttered slowly.

"Oh, Martina I must go away. I cannot stay here on this yacht with either Hugh or Robin."

"You are right. Neither of us can. We have to leave at once. We can jump on the train to Nice and then catch a train from there to – anywhere. We don't have to return to

England, we can travel for a while and nobody will know where we are. But we must escape."

Escape, *escape*. The word pounded in her brain. Hugh was married to Harriet and she could not stay near him, loving him so. It would break her heart to leave him, but it must be done.

"Shall I come with you?" Kitty asked. "You'll need me if you're travelling."

"Yes, we will," Martina agreed distractedly. "Then you had better know everything."

Briefly she explained about the double 'wedding' and the confusion. Kitty wasted no time with exclamations, but nodded sympathetically and said,

"I will pack some things."

"Not too much," Martina said. "We must travel light. While you're doing that, I must write a letter."

She hurried next door before her emotion overcame her. She sat down and tried to calm herself enough to write her farewell to Hugh.

"Dearest Hugh,

I love you and I always will. But while there is any chance that you and Harriet are married, I cannot stay near you.

Harriet is coming with me and perhaps there is some way that you can sort out this mess, so that both of you can be free again. Then maybe there is hope for us and one day we can be together. I shall pray for that day with all my heart. But in the meantime, we must be apart.

Goodbye, my dearest, dearest love. I shall never forget you or stop loving you.

Your own true,

Martina."

She had brought the marriage certificate with her.

Now she placed it in the envelope with the letter, sealed it and then dropped her head onto it in a passion of sobbing.

She dried her tears as Kitty came in to start packing some clothes for her and left the letter propped up against the mirror. Hugh would find it when he searched for her.

At last they were ready. Quietly they made their way to the gangway and slipped down it like shadows. Nobody saw them.

They began to walk in the direction of the station. As the road began to slope uphill, Martina turned and looked back at the ship where she had known such brief and intense happiness.

Tears poured down her cheeks again.

It was all over. She had spoken of 'one day', but in her heart she knew that 'one day' would never come.

She would never see Hugh again, never kiss him, never tell him what he meant to her. And it was only at this moment that she knew how totally, completely and passionately she loved him.

"Goodbye, my love," she whispered through her tears. *"Goodbye, goodbye."*

CHAPTER TEN

It was two hours later that Hugh and Robin returned to the yacht. Robin's angry mood had subsided and now he was quiet and slightly shame-faced.

"If only my temper hadn't got the better of me," he mourned. "I should have listened while you explained how matters really stood."

"Yes, you should," Hugh agreed with a grin.

"I must say, Hugh, you played a dashed clever trick."

"Hmm! A sight too clever for my own good. What Martina will say when I have to confess all, I do not know. Or rather, I *do* know."

"And you have not yet told her?"

"I couldn't. At first I thought it would be easy, but then I came to see that she might be angry that I had deceived her somewhat. Now I am wondering if she will ever forgive me."

"And I am afraid that Harriet will never forgive me," Robin added. "I said such terrible things."

"Of course she will forgive you. She loves you a great deal better than you deserve."

Hugh stood on the quiet deck and looked around him.

"They are probably both asleep," he said. "Shall we wait until morning before telling them everything or dare we wake them up now?"

"They might not be asleep," Robin observed. "We could venture to knock on their doors."

Together they went below and Hugh rapped gently on Martina's door. When there was no reply he knocked again louder.

Robin tried Harriet's door but again there was silence.

"There must both be asleep," Hugh said.

"Yes, of course."

But an uneasiness had descended on both men. Neither of them felt able to march into a lady's bedroom, but they were troubled.

"Kitty," Hugh suggested. "She can go in."

He headed for Kitty's room and knocked. Again there was silence. Taking a deep breath Hugh turned the knob and looked in.

There was light coming through the porthole and he knew at once that Kitty was not there. His unease was growing by the second.

He determined to chance it. Knocking once more on Martina's door and receiving no reply, he opened the door.

"She's not there," he reported grimly, as he emerged. "Now we'll have to check on Harriet's cabin."

But the moonlight falling on the pillow had shown Hugh the letter. He reached out to take it and stood holding it, not trying to open it.

"Leave me a moment," he requested.

"Hugh, what – ?"

"I said leave me," he repeated with soft violence.

Robin backed out, leaving Hugh still staring at the envelope.

At last he lit a lamp and sat on the bed. As he read the letter a stillness came over him, until at last his shoulders sagged and he let his head fall forward.

"My God!" he whispered. "What have I done? How could I have been so stupid as not to tell her and prevent all this?"

Moving slowly, like a man who had received a stunning blow, he left the cabin to find Robin.

"What is it?" Robin asked, alarmed at the sight of his face.

Hugh handed him the marriage certificate.

"It seems that Harriet accidentally signed her own name and now they think that she and I are married. So they have run away to put distance between us."

"You mean they've left the yacht?"

"So it seems. Let's find out if anyone saw them."

"If they left the ship, sir, it was without informing me," the Captain asserted. "I hope you do not feel that I was at fault in any way."

"Not at all," Hugh said at once. "If they were determined to slip away unnoticed, there is nothing you could have done. Indeed, there is nothing you could have done even if you had known, for you could hardly have stopped them."

"Does the maid know anything, Sir Hugh?"

"She is missing too."

"How far can they have gone?" Robin demanded.

"Not far. They will have made for the railway station, in which case, we can still catch them."

"Then let's hurry."

As one man they turned and headed for the gangway.

"*Sir Hugh!*"

At the top of the gangway they stopped, arrested by a shriek from somewhere in the harbour.

"*Sir Hugh!*"

"There!" Robin shouted, pointing to a figure that was flying down the road screaming.

"It's Kitty," Hugh exclaimed after a moment. "And she's alone."

They hurried down to meet Kitty on the quay.

She was distraught, her hair flying in the breeze, her clothes dishevelled.

"Sir Hugh," she gasped, almost collapsing into his arms.

"Kitty, whatever is the matter?" he enquired, steadying her. "Where are your Mistresses?"

"They took them, sir. Oh, sir, they carried them off."

"*What?* Tell me everything."

Inwardly he was terrified by what he had heard, but he forced himself to be calm.

"We were walking to the station, sir, and two men jumped out at us. They seized the misses and kidnapped them. I was just a bit behind and I don't think they saw me, so I managed to slip away around the corner.

"I didn't go far because I thought I could find out where they were going. I crept after them and heard what they said."

"And what did they say?" Hugh asked in agony.

"Something about money," Kitty gasped. "They knew Miss Lawson had made a big win at the casino."

"Of course they did," Hugh groaned. "She told the whole world while we were coming back to the yacht."

"And made herself a target," Robin moaned.

"Whoever they are, they must have followed our carriage until they saw her go aboard," Hugh agreed. "Then they hid and waited their chance. They probably couldn't believe their luck when they left with no male escort. But Kitty you said they had taken them away somewhere."

"Yes, Sir Hugh. They were just going to rob them at first, but then one said they could ask ransom from the owner of such a fine ship."

"Did you see where they went?"

"Part of the way, sir. Then I lost them."

"Take us as far as you can."

Hugh turned to the Captain who had come down to the quay and was listening.

"Send someone to the Police Station to bring back help. In the meantime I want as many able-bodied men as you can spare."

The Captain hurried away. Hugh looked at Kitty with concern.

"My poor girl," he said, "you must be exhausted. Have you the strength to come with us?"

"Oh, yes, sir. I couldn't rest until the ladies are safe. They have been so good to me and I want to help them."

In a few minutes the Captain returned, followed by several crew members.

"Every single man wanted to come," he said. "I have just left enough on board to man the ship."

Kitty had recovered her breath and was ready to lead on. They all followed her up the road from the quay.

"It was just here," she informed them as they turned a corner. "They seized my ladies just over there and took them away down that street."

"One man must remain here to direct the Police," Hugh ordered. "The rest of us come this way."

They headed off down the road and Kitty led them right to the end. From there she was able to show them another road, but at the end of it she became lost. There were two turnings.

"I didn't see which one they took," she admitted in despair. "I'd lost them by then."

"All right," Hugh said. "You've done very well, Kitty. "We will split into two parties and each take one turning."

But the divide was an illusion as the two streets met again a hundred yards further on.

"They could have taken them into one of these houses," Robin muttered.

"Or onto a boat," Hugh suggested suddenly. "The ground is sloping down. This must be another way down to the harbour."

"Then they might already be out to sea," Robin said aghast.

"Don't panic. They will not have set sail if they are hoping for a ransom."

"Hallo there, Sir Hugh!"

It was the crewman who had gone for the Police and he was accompanied by several hefty looking gendarmes.

Briefly and in faultless French, Hugh explained the situation and the chief among them, a stern authoritative man said,

"We know these men. We have been trying to catch them because they give the whole place a bad name. If you can help us you will have done everyone a service."

Together they all headed down to the harbour.

Suddenly Kitty stopped.

"There," she said urgently.

She was pointing through the window of a tavern, where a man was sitting drinking ale.

"That's one of them, I am sure of it."

"Let me get to him," Robin exclaimed, launching himself forward.

He was restrained by both the Policemen and Hugh.

"Be silent, you idiot," Hugh snapped. "We must wait until he comes out and then follow him."

They did not have long to wait. Ten minutes later the man rose and walked towards the door. They all pressed back into the shadows as he emerged and paused a moment before setting off in the direction of the harbour.

He walked for some distance away from the luxurious yachts like Hugh's in the direction of smaller vessels.

They followed him at a distance.

At last he turned sharply in the direction of a small boat shabbier than the others.

"Can they really be here?" Robin breathed. "How monstrous."

As soon as the man disappeared, they crept down closer to the boat. There they paused.

"We should proceed carefully," the Policeman advised. "As many of us as possible should sneak aboard before they know we're here."

At that moment they heard a woman's scream from the boat. That finished all caution. Hugh leapt onto the boat closely followed by Robin and with the sailors and Police hurrying after them.

Hugh tore through the ship like a madman, calling Martina's name.

At last he thought he could hear his own name called in a distant voice. It seemed to be coming from under a hatch.

He and Robin wrenched at the hatch and finally managed to pull it open, but they could see only darkness beneath.

"Martina!" Hugh shouted.

"I am here," came a faint voice.

"Harriet," Robin screamed down into the hole.

"Oh, Robin, Robin."

Someone shone a lamp down into the hold and by its faint glow they could just see the two girls huddled together on a pile of sacks.

With an oath Hugh shinned down the ladder followed by Robin. In another moment he held Martina in his arms.

"My darling," he cried fiercely, "thank God you are safe. How could you run away from me like that?"

"But I had to," she whispered. "Didn't you get my letter?"

"Yes, and you are wrong. I am not married to Harriet. I never was. Hush! I will explain it all later. For now it's enough that I have found you and I will never let you go."

"Hold me," she gasped. "I have been *so* frightened."

"Let me get you out of here quickly."

He helped her up the ladder followed by Harriet and Robin. The gendarmes had just finished rounding up everyone on board.

"It's a magnificent night's work," the chief gendarme was saying. "Thanks to all of you. I should really ask you to come with me to the Police Station, but perhaps you had better leave that until morning. By then, hopefully, the ladies will have recovered."

They thanked him gratefully. All they wanted now was to be alone.

Some of the crew had secured two cabs to take them back to the ship. Robin and Harriet climbed into one, Martina and Hugh into the other.

At once Hugh took Martina into his arms, holding her

closely in a passion of thankfulness that she had been restored safely to him.

"My love, my dearest," he murmured between kisses. "What would I have done if I had lost you?"

"Dearest Hugh, I was so afraid. I thought I would die without seeing you again."

"You should never have gone. Harriet and I are not married. There is nothing to keep us apart."

"But the certificate in her name – "

"Dearest Martina, try to forgive me for my deception. I meant it innocently. That 'certificate' is just a meaningless piece of paper. There was *no* marriage."

"But the priest – "

"There was no priest. The old man was a doctor before he retired to a cottage on my estate. He was delighted to help me. He always wanted to be an actor.

"And even if he had been a priest, the Chapel was deconsecrated many years ago and no marriages can be performed there. The whole wedding is totally null and void."

"But – the letter you wrote to the Archbishop?"

"That simply contained a donation to Church funds. Despite what I said, the letter made no mention of any marriage."

Martina stared at him dumbfounded. It gave him time to say quickly,

"Forgive me, my dearest. I had to do it. I knew your plan was wild and impossible from the first moment. There were so many things that could go wrong and ensnare us in scandal for the rest of our lives.

"I had to think of something quickly. I could not refuse you in case you thought of an even madder plan. Or went to somebody else. And besides – "

"Besides?"

"I could not resist the chance to take you away with me on my yacht and have you all to myself for a while. I believed we would grow closer and perhaps I could win your love. And then I would be able to admit everything to you."

"But why didn't you?" she asked in wonder.

"Because you made it impossible for me. Do you remember that night in Gibraltar when we walked together and you said I was the most honest man alive and you could trust me absolutely?

"You said, 'you would never tell me you were doing one thing and then do another.' If you only knew how those words made my heart sink, because that was exactly what I *was* doing.

"And you said that if I deceived you, you would mind more with me than with anyone else. That finished me. There was no way I could make my confession after that remark."

Martina stared at him stricken.

"My darling Hugh, it is I who should ask forgiveness of you. I showed you no understanding. Of course I do not blame you for what you did.

"You were right and you have saved us all from a terrible misfortune. In future, I promise never to think of any more clever plans, but always to be guided by you."

"No, don't do that," he retorted quickly. "If you were meek and dutiful I would not recognise you. Just be your own true wonderful self and that is all I ask. Just say that you are not angry with me?"

"How can I be angry when I love you so much?"

"My darling!" he cried and swept her into his arms.

They stayed locked in an embrace until they reached the quay. As they left the cab, the sailors, who had returned on foot, now appeared in the distance running. They cheered as they saw the couples and ran even faster.

"Thank you, thank you," Martina cried as they neared and the others echoed her.

Still cheering, the sailors followed them aboard. The chef was there, urging them to go to the saloon where he would provide refreshments.

"I would so love a cup of tea," Martina said eagerly.

When they were sitting comfortably in the saloon she quizzed,

"How did you find us? We knew Kitty had gone for help, but we didn't see how you could track us down to that dreadful boat."

"Kitty followed you for quite a distance," Hugh explained. "She managed to take us part of the way and next she spotted one of the men in a tavern and identified him. Then we only had to follow him. My darling, however did they get you onto that terrible boat?"

"We were going to the railway station and they just jumped out on us. They seized our purses and I thought they just meant to take our money. But then they said they would hold us for ransom.

"When they took us onto the boat I thought they meant to sail out to sea and hold us there. We were so afraid. But they only threw us into the hold and left us in darkness."

She shuddered at the memory and Hugh sat beside her, taking her in his arms again.

"I would dearly love to sail away from here," he said. "But we cannot do that. We must help the Police to ensure that those fellows are put away for a very long time."

"And while we are staying here," Robin announced, "Harriet and I are going to be married. I have begged her forgiveness for the way I behaved, and my darling has promised to be mine."

Hugh said nothing, but he kissed Martina's hand. She understood. He would not speak of their love before the others.

He watched her with tender, possessive eyes as she drank her tea and managed to eat something. Then he took her hand and drew her to her feet.

"That is all for tonight," Hugh said. "We shall all have much to discuss in the morning."

He carried her down to her cabin and took her inside. There he set her on the bed and sat beside her taking her hand in his.

"I have loved you," he said, "so completely that, as far as I am concerned, no other woman exists in the world but you. I want you! I love you and my whole life depends on you. But I only want you, if you want me."

"You know that I want you," Martina sighed. "I took too long to realise my love for you, but it is real true love. Nothing else in the whole world is as important to me – as you."

She only whispered the last words but Hugh still heard them.

His hand tightened on hers. Then he said very quietly,

"I can only thank God that by some miracle He has brought us together again."

"I thought you would forget me," Martina breathed.

"I could never forget you," Hugh told her. "I believe we were meant for each other from the moment we were born.

"I adore you, Martina, and I worship you. If you are mine, I am the happiest man on earth."

He spoke very quietly. Then he kissed her.

For a moment as their lips met, there was only softness and gentleness.

As if Hugh wanted to make her his completely and absolutely, he put his arms round her and kissed her until she felt as if she had become part of him.

'I love you! I love you,' she wanted to say, but it was impossible to speak.

She felt as he continued kissing her, as if he was carrying her up into Heaven.

When she could finally speak again she told him,

"I will make up for all the time you have lost. I love you! I love you, as I have never loved anyone in my entire life."

"And you must go on loving me," Hugh urged. "I have lived without you for what seems an eternity and once you are mine, I will never never lose you."

"I feel no one could be as happy as I am at this very moment," Martina whispered.

Hugh tried to put his feelings into words, but no words were deep enough. So he kissed her yet again until they were both breathless.

"I adore you," he murmured as she fell back against the pillows. "Now I am going to leave you but I will dream about you all night and soon we will be married."

"I love you with all my heart and all my soul," she declared. "I think together we will find a Heaven of our own which will be ours until we leave this earth inseparable for Heaven itself."

There was nothing more Hugh could say.

He only smiled at her, the smile of a totally happy and complete man and she knew that she possessed his heart and his soul for eternity.

It was as if the stars and the moon were telling them how happy they were and how they must never lose their love for each other as such love comes only from God and the Divine.